THE LOST PUNCH
THE COMPLETE CASES OF GILLIAN
HAZELTINE, VOLUME 4

BOOKS IN THE ARGOSY LIBRARY:

UP JUMPED THE DEVIL
CLEVE F. ADAMS

THE BROTHERS OF THE SNAKE: THE
COMPLETE CHINATOWN CASES OF
JIMMY WENTWORTH, VOLUME 3
SIDNEY HERSCHEL SMALL

A CLUE TO THE COPPER: THE COMPLETE
CASES OF SILVER SKULL
RICHARD HOWELLS WATKINS

KINGDOM OF THE LOST: THE ADVENTURES
OF PETER THE BRAZEN, VOLUME 8
LORING BRENT

WORTH MILLIONS
RICHARD BARRY

TIGER DICK'S DOUBLOONS
DON MCGREW

PRESIDENTS: IMAGINARY MOMENTS IN
THE LIVES OF AMERICA'S GREAT
THEODORE ROSCOE

CROSS OVER NINE
MAX BRAND

ASOKA'S ALIBI: THE COMPLETE
ADVENTURES OF BEN QUORN, VOLUME 2
TALBOT MUNDY

THE LOST PUNCH: THE COMPLETE CASES
OF GILLIAN HAZELTINE, VOLUME 4
GEORGE F. WORTS

THE LOST PUNCH
THE COMPLETE CASES OF
GILLIAN HAZELTINE, VOLUME 4

GEORGE F. WORTS

ILLUSTRATED BY
ROGER B. MORRISON

COVER BY
HOWARD V. BROWN

POPULAR PUBLICATIONS · 2025

TABLE OF CONTENTS

A REPTILE NAMED ROBARD

*Blackmail winds its tentacles around
Gillian Hazeltine and his friends as
the great criminal lawyer tries to save
what is nearest and dearest to him*

1

OVERHEARD

GILLIAN HAZELTINE, SOMETIMES referred to by his enemies as the Silver Fox—and not entirely because Gillian's thick, curly black hair was sprinkled with silver—sat on a bench in the locker room of the Greenboro Country Club with a Scotch highball in his hand and listened to voices of treachery. On the bench beside the famous criminal lawyer sat one of his closest friends, Victor Henshaw, owner and publisher of the Greenboro *Morning Times*.

The criminal lawyer and the newspaper publisher had finished eighteen holes, had had their showers and now, half-dressed, were prepared to hold an amiable post-mortem on their game. But that post-mortem was destined never to be held. As they sat there, lazily tinkling the ice in their glasses, voices floated in at the window above them.

The window was open and it was screened with new copper mesh. Gillian would remember that new copper mesh for a long time. It was so new that it gleamed like a web of gold. And the voice, the first voice, that came through it was a voice of gold. It was the voice of Gillian's wife, Vee-Anne; a clear, sweet voice, and it was agitated.

"No, Don, no—please," said the voice of Gillian's wife.

Gillian flashed a look at his friend. Involuntarily, Gillian smiled. That clear, sweet, golden voice usually made him

3

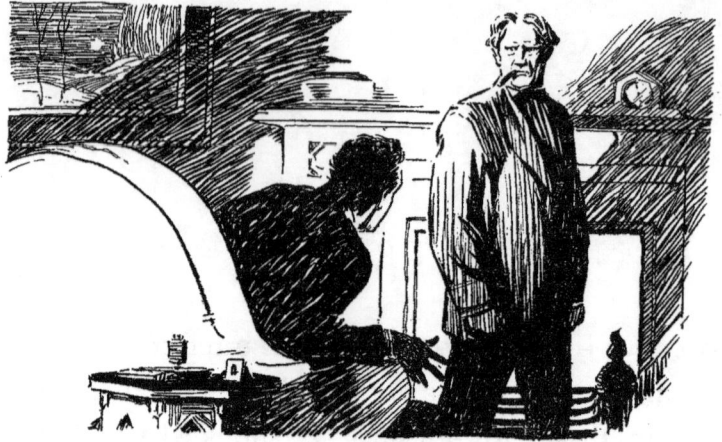

"That's what I said—I'm going to commit suicide"

smile indulgently, for Gillian made no bones about the fact that he was madly in love with his wife.

Victor Henshaw's face made Gillian's smile widen. Victor Henshaw's face was that of a lion. It was, in that respect, almost a comical face. Just now it was pinkly aglow from exercise and the stinging cold shower. It was surmounted by a mane of tawny hair. The amber eyes were fierce like those of a lion. And somehow the publisher's face was leonine, with deep grooves running down from the pudgy nose and bracketing the mouth.

The publisher did not see Gillian's smile. With shaggy tan brows bunched together, he was staring at the drink in his hand.

Outside the window another voice made itself heard. It was a man's voice, deep and resonant and rich, with musical overtones and undertones. Even if his wife had not called the man by name, Gillian would have identified him by that rich, resonant voice as Don Robard, a fellow club member.

"I will expect you at my apartment at nine to-night."

Gillian was slow to grasp the significance of those words, perhaps because his mind was in a state of dreamy repose. The golf game, which he had won from Victor Henshaw, the invigorating shower, the illegal but ambrosial highball, and, finally, the golden voice of his wife had placed him in a delightfully harmonious mood.

The voice of Don Robard sent his mind wandering before the man's words took on meaning. Don Robard had always been, to Gillian, a mysterious and somewhat romantic figure; a man who lived an enviable life. From some source he enjoyed an income sufficiently generous so that it was unnecessary for him to soil his slender, artistic hands or to tire his brain with toil in any form.

"I will expect you at my apartment at nine to-night." THOSE WORDS WERE still tumbling about meaninglessly in Gillian's brain. He was recalling that Don Robard, when not traveling or hunting, was generally to be seen, an attractive figure, playing polo recklessly, playing golf brilliantly. A darkly handsome man, he was tremendously attractive to women.

Gillian shook his head slightly as the voice of his wife spoke again. It was the timbre of her voice that aroused him. She was nervous—frightened. He knew that tone well.

"No, Don—please!"

"At nine," said Don Robard.

"What can I tell my husband?"

"Anything you wish, my dear—what you've told him before."

That was all. The voices drifted off beyond earshot. Such

of the conversation as Gillian had overheard had taken less than twenty seconds. And it took Gillian Hazeltine that long to come fully to his senses. His wife's voice, strained, pleading, still rang in his ears. And the voice of Don Robard rang, too—a knell.

Gillian raised an uncertain hand to his forehead, and found that it was dripping with sweat. His other hand, containing the highball, was trembling so that some of the amber liquid spilled out upon the cement floor.

But even with the shock of that conversation upon him, he was able to be astonished by the startling change that had come over Victor Henshaw. Following that conversation, the newspaper publisher had turned deathly white. He had hurriedly placed his highball on the bench beside him. Now he was gripping the edge of the bench with both hands, as if to save himself from toppling over. His lips were skinned back tightly from his teeth. His eyes were shut so tightly that the skin about them was blue.

Gillian, with some difficulty, cleared his throat and said in a thick, unsteady voice, "Well!"

Victor Henshaw slowly opened his eyes and looked at Gillian. They were bloodshot and there was a ferocity in them that Gillian had never before seen in human eyes. The expression, indeed, was not human. It was that of a fighting animal at bay. That expression should have been accompanied by a deep-chested snarl—the snarl of a challenge to combat.

The newspaper publisher said harshly:

"When a heel descends on a snake, one of several things may happen. The snake may whip about and sink its fangs into the heel. Or it may crawl away, wounded, to die or recover. Or the descent of the heel may instantly kill it, unless there is something in the old superstition that no snake actually dies until the sun has set."

"Don Robard," said Gillian.

Victor Henshaw reached for his highball and gulped it. Gillian watched him with an almost detached curiosity. Don Robard—a snake. Yes; that was apparently true. Too much was happening for Gillian. He was a man of stout heart, of lightning-quick brain. Time after time he had performed legal miracles in court rooms—performed mental feats at crucial moments which had left his enemies breathless in defeat. But in the face of this personal calamity he could not think or act. He was helpless.

In heavy silence, the two men finished dressing. Victor Henshaw was the first to finish. He made quite a business of closing his locker and adjusting his new Panama with its gay blue-and-white band. He bit the end off of a long dark cigar, lighted it and puffed at it. He said presently:

"Gillian, I will call at your house at nine o'clock to-night. I have something to tell you. As my attorney and as my friend, I must have your advice on a tremendously important matter. It concerns—a reptile named Robard."

WHEN GILLIAN LEFT the locker room to join his wife on the clubhouse veranda, he had himself fairly well in hand. He was determined to betray none of the feelings which were attacking him like so much acid. There was, he had begun to be certain, some mistake—he had placed the obvious, the wrong construction on what he had overheard. There would be a simple and amusing explanation. Yet why had Vic Henshaw been so vehement, "A reptile named Robard!"

Mrs. Hazeltine was waiting for Gillian, and she was alone, sipping a lemonade. And it seemed to Gillian that she had never been so beautiful. In a blue summer dress, she was small, slim—a charming young woman. A trail of tiny freckles across her little tip-tilted nose made her seem girlish. She was wearing no hat and her hair gleamed—as that new copper mesh had gleamed. It was red, that hair— the reddest hair that Gillian had ever seen. And her eyes were green. Not the green that can be mistaken for blue, but the green of the Ceylon emerald.

Gillian came toward her smiling. He was reputed to be a great actor, when the occasion called for it, in the court room. He was a great actor now. His smile was warm, indulging, affectionate. He saw it chase a ghost of trouble out of her eyes.

Mrs. Hazeltine said: "Have a good game, dear?"

"Swell game."

"Tell me all about it. Let's drive home by the river road."

He told her about the game on the way to the car and on the drive home. He always tried to make his adventures on the links, in the office and in the court room sound amusing, because he liked to hear her laugh. Like her voice, it was a golden laugh. His ears, sensitized by suspicion, detected a strained note in her laughter this afternoon.

A reptile named Robard!

As they hummed along the river road in the new roadster he had given her on her last birthday, Gillian casually asked her if she had met any interesting people this afternoon.

"Nobody but you, darling."

Gillian chuckled; waited for her to mention Don

Robard. But she did not. She discussed what she had planned for his supper.

"We'll have it out on the terrace, dearest—an early supper, if you don't mind."

Gillian mustered his fondest smile and waited. He had the feeling of being alone, shut out, in a hostile world. Heretofore, he and his wife had shared their most intimate secrets. To him, she had always been a refuge. Being of a romantic turn of mind, Gillian considered his home his fortress. In it, he was safe from the hurts, the disappointments of the world.

"I have to run an errand after supper," his wife easily explained.

Gillian's heart leaped with hope. She would now explain Don Robard. And it would be a beautifully simple explanation that would restore his faith. But what she said was:

"Gladys Mandelle wants me to run over for a few minutes around nine o'clock—something about a new dress."

"Want me to go along?"

"I wouldn't dream of it, darling. I know how you hate Ed Mandelle—and how Gladys bores you. No; I'll drive over alone. I'll be back by ten."

"Very well," said Gillian, matching her carelessness.

IT WAS HALF past eight when they finished supper. Vee-Anne liked to eat by candlelight, but the candles were extinguished because of the insects they attracted. The only light was starlight and the glow, waxing and waning like a distant and eccentric volcano, of Gillian's perfecto.

He was unprepared when Vee-Anne left her chair, came over and kissed him lightly on the cheek. His heart said:

"She's going to him now." But his voice calmly inquired: "Going now, dear?"

"I'll be back soon."

"Sure you don't want me to drive you over?"

"I wouldn't dream of inflicting the Mandelles on you!"

She went so softly that he did not hear her.

Gillian waited patiently until the sound of the starter came to him from the garage: watched the twin beams of its headlights sweeping like beacons across the shrubbery bordering the driveway, and heard the purr of the exhaust and the crunching of tires on gravel as it went down the hill and into Riverside Avenue.

His heart was beating rapidly. He suddenly felt cold and sick all over. How long, he wondered, had this hypocrisy been going on? What a fool he had been!

An old superstition instantly recurred to him: red-headed women had almost always brought him bad luck. He had thought, until this afternoon, that this redhead had brought him the greatest luck and the greatest happiness he had ever known.

And his pride would permit him to do nothing about it. If she wanted Robard, she could have Robard, and he would not lift a finger to interfere.

It was one of his fixed beliefs that if a man cannot hold a woman by love, he is a fool trying to hold her.

A reptile named Robard! Not a reptile—an owl. Strangely, Don Robard's face had always reminded Gillian of an owl. The round, vigilant eyes set in dark round sockets; the slightly hooked nose; the eyebrows always arched as if in surprise.

Victor Henshaw had said: "The snake may whip about and sink its fangs into the heel."

Gillian sprang up and went into the house. He ascended to his study on the second floor, switched on the lights and looked at the little clock on his desk. It was nine five. She would be there now—with Robard. In that luxurious bachelor's apartment in the Herrendon Arms. Men sometimes grinned slyly when that apartment was mentioned.

Gillian seated himself at his desk and watched the hands of the little silver clock.

Slowly they crept to nine ten, to nine fifteen.

It was nine twenty when Gillian's houseman, Toro, a Japanese of infinite wisdom and of amazing understanding, entered on silent feet and announced:

"Mr. Victor Henshaw is downstairs, sir."

"Tell him," said Gillian, "I'll be down immediately."

When Toro was gone, Gillian snatched the telephone receiver from its hook. She had had ample time. He called the Mandelle's number. A woman's voice answered, the throaty, full voice of Gladys Mandelle.

"This is Gillian, Gladys. Vee-Anne isn't there, by any chance, is she?"

"Vee-Anne? Why, no, Gillian. Was she coming here this evening?"

"I must have misunderstood her. She was stopping to see somebody about a dress, and I thought it might have been you."

"I'm certain it couldn't be me, Gillian. I saw her at the club this afternoon, and she would have mentioned it."

Gillian thanked her, said good-by amiably, and hung up. So she was lying, after all!

She would be in Don Robard's arms now.

Feeling more than a little faint, Gillian descended the stairs and entered the living room.

2

TRAIL OF THE SNAKE

THE OWNER AND publisher of the Greenboro *Morning Times* was standing with his back to the empty fireplace, his elbows hooked up on the low mantel. A strand of his tawny mane had fallen forward over one eye. A cigar was clamped in one corner of his mouth. His amber eyes swept fiercely over Gillian's white face.

He said, "Well, Gil?" sharply.

Gillian glanced away and shrugged.

Victor Henshaw said: "Did she go?"

"Yes."

Henshaw removed his elbows from the mantel and said in his harsh voice: "Something has got to be done about that man. Something drastic has got to be done."

Gillian dropped down in a deeply upholstered armchair. He was conscious of resentment at having this painful situation discussed, even by a friend as close to him as was Victor Henshaw.

He said curtly: "You wanted my advice, Vic, on a legal matter."

"I wanted your legal and personal advice on the matter of Don Robard."

"How does he concern you?"

Vic Henshaw gazed at him thoughtfully. "I don't suppose you even suspect."

Gillian shook his head.

"I'll tell you a little story to make it clear. Do you remember when I came to Greenboro? No, you were too young. I am forty-nine. You must be thirty-five or six. I came to Greenboro when I was twenty-nine. It must have been a pathetic picture, Gil. Even now I can look back and feel sorry for that young man who came into this town with his year-old baby daughter in his arms. No one knew where I came from—and no one cared a damn. I had seven dollars in my pocket and a year-old baby on my hands."

"Dorothy," Gillian murmured.

"Yes. Her mother died when she was born. You knew, of course, that I came from the West."

Gillian nodded. "I vaguely remember." And his mind returned to that luxurious apartment in the Herrendon Arms. He heard Vic Henshaw's voice, but the words were nothing but sounds that rose and fell, stopped and began again.

"I have tried to keep it very vague. I have taken pains to build up a background, an early beginning, of unimportance. I have simply been a poor, unimportant man from California who came to Greenboro and made a fortune in the newspaper business. I managed to drown out all interest in my youth by my rise to success. You know that story, of course—how I started in the pressroom of the old *Times* and worked up until I became managing editor, then editor, then publisher and finally sole owner."

Gillian knew only from the sound of his friend's voice that an affirmative answer was expected. He nodded.

"That story, I believe," Henshaw went on, "is held up as a powerful moral lesson to Greenboro young men about to start forth to make the world their oyster. There isn't a blot on that record. I am proud of it!"

THE NEWSPAPER OWNER glared at Gillian and harshly added:

"But what does it profit a man— No, I don't mean that. I profited by early mistakes and made of my paper a strong force for good in this community. You know that."

"Oh, yes. Yes, Vic."

"You aren't hearing a word I say! Listen to me. This is not an aimless reminiscence. I tell you that my life may hinge on what you advise me to do to-night. Gillian, I am planning to commit suicide!"

It was as effective as a bucket of ice water thrown in Gillian's face. His eyes cleared. His mouth lost its droop and became firm. He repeated sharply, "Suicide?"

"That's what I said. I'm going to commit suicide. There's no way out of it. I want to make sure that my house is in order. I want to make sure that my daughter will be protected in every way. There will be no scandal."

"This," said Gillian, "is absolutely absurd. Only cowards talk of committing suicide, Victor."

"I disagree with you, but we won't discuss it. You know that I am interested in aviation, that I am taking flying lessons at the municipal airport. I am already soloing. I am going up in my plane and I am going to put it into a tailspin. I am not going to pull the ship out of that spin. It is," he added ironically, "a somewhat more original method than jumping out of a twelve story window or putting the barrel of a shotgun in your mouth and your toe on the trigger."

"Why suicide?" Gillian grated.

"Did it ever occur to you to wonder," the newspaper owner asked, "from what source Don Robard's handsome income is derived?"

"Isn't he independently wealthy?"

"Yes. But from what source?"

"Supposing you tell me."

"I am the source! No, it never occurred to you. It never occurred to anybody to wonder how he is able to support himself in that sybaritic apartment, how he is able to support a string of a dozen polo ponies, how he is able to travel and hunt and entertain and, in every way, to lead the life of a man with a huge income. I supply that income. For fifteen years, Gillian, that leech has bled me."

"Blackmail," said Gillian.

"Blood money!"

Gillian nodded gloomily. His brain was clear now. "Tell me about it."

Victor Henshaw walked over from the fireplace and seated himself in a chair beside the criminal lawyer. He placed his hand on Gillian's knee. There was no ferocity in his eyes now. They were desperate with suffering.

"When I was twenty-one I killed a man. It was a barroom brawl. There were no extenuating circumstances. We were playing poker. We were both drunk. It happened in a water front dive on the old Barbary Coast in San Francisco. His name doesn't matter. He was a wharf rat. To this day I am certain he cheated and that he was steal-ing money out of the pot. Again, no matter. I have never tried to excuse myself. There was a great deal of confusion. We were on our feet shouting names at each other. There was a beer bottle in my hand. I hit him with that bottle. It killed him."

THE NEWSPAPER PUBLISHER stopped. He produced a large hand-monogrammed linen handkerchief and mopped his forehead. Then he blew his nose. He went on:

"I was given ten years on a second degree manslaughter charge. Good behavior cut that down to seven. When I got out I married the girl to whom I had been engaged. She had waited. She was that kind."

Victor Henshaw paused again.

"Robard?" Gillian prompted him.

"Was a son of one of the wardens. I wore a beard in those days. No, they didn't make me shave it off. That beard probably saved my life. If it hadn't been for that beard, there would have been a hundred Don Robards. When they let me out, I shaved off the beard. When my wife died, I worked until I had saved enough to come east. By pure chance I came to Greenboro. I liked Greenboro. I wanted to live here, forget my past and build up a future to be proud of."

Again Victor Henshaw stopped.

"Fifteen years ago, I was just beginning to find my way, just beginning to see my dreams turn into reality, when Don Robard came to town. To this day I do not know whether he traced me or whether he stumbled upon me accidentally. In any event he knew me—and he called me by my old, my real name. Since then I have been paying him to keep his mouth shut. Gillian, I have lain awake night after night planning to murder that man. But I can't murder him. When I see him talking to my daughter, mingling with my friends, even in my own house eating my food and drinking my wine—I could take his neck in my hands and strangle him. I've come to know what hatred is, and what hell is! So, you see, I'm a Dr. Jekyll and Mr. Hyde—on one hand, a high-moraled pillar of the community, and on the other an actual and a potential murderer."

"So," Gillian stated bluntly, "is every man."

"Not every man has actually committed a murder."

"Any man would be justified in killing Robard."

The amber leonine eyes stared at Gillian. Gillian wondered if he saw a furtive hope glowing in their depths. And he slowly shook his head. The newspaper publisher lighted a fresh cigar. He said, in the same deep voice:

"There is nothing to be gained by beating about the bush, Gillian. I had hoped that you might suggest some way of removing that reptile."

"Some way," Gillian agreed, "other than murder. A great many ugly stories are in circulation concerning me. My enemies say that I will stoop to anything to further my ends. I have been accused of using lying witnesses, of buying judges and of bribing juries. I have even been accused of hiring gunmen."

"All," said Victor Henshaw in his harsh voice, "in the sacred name of justice."

"I deal out justice," Gillian defended himself, "with an iron hand. The deplorable state of our courts makes it necessary. Yes, Victor, I have stooped low in dispensing my brand of justice—making certain that the guilty are punished and the innocent are freed—but I have never been a party to a murder."

The publisher fastened his fierce amber eyes on Gillian.

"I have a file of your activities in my private archives," he said. "If it were made public, it would disbar you and send you to the penitentiary for six hundred years!"

GILLIAN'S SMILE WAS one of mock dismay.

"Don't tell me you're going to blackmail me!"

But the publisher did not smile. He whipped out: "I tell you, Gillian, I am desperate!"

"As desperate as you are, and as unpleasant as it is to fork out hush money to Robard, isn't that pleasanter than the prospect of suicide? Why must you commit suicide? Why don't you continue paying Robard?"

Victor Henshaw glared. "Is that sound, legal advice?"

"No. It is merely a question. Why must you commit suicide?"

"Because I am desperate. Last year I paid to Robard approximately a fourth of my income. He has increased his demands. He now insists that I sign over to him a half interest in the *Times*. If I do not do it, he will blab."

"He is bluffing."

"He is not bluffing. And if I sign over to him that half interest, I will lose what I have worked for the past twenty years. I will not care to live, because the *Times* is my life."

Gillian gloomily shook his head.

"You should try bluffing him."

"I have tried it. You do not seem to understand. That man hates me as a beggar hates the man who gives him alms. One way or another, he is determined to ruin me. I would rather kill myself than let him succeed."

"There must," said Gillian, "be some alternative."

"There is one. It, too, is a form of suicide. My tailspin

would kill me bodily. The alternative would kill me as a public figure—but it would be revenge. And there is a chance that it might not kill me publicly. The public might acclaim me."

Victor Henshaw hunched forward in his chair.

"I have the story written," he proceeded. "It is the true story of my life. In that story I have told of the murder I committed, of my years in the penitentiary, of my life here—and of Don Robard. My plan is to devote the entire front page of the *Times* some morning to this exposure of my past. I present the facts, without emotion and without prejudice. I throw myself on the mercy of my readers, the public. I have almost convinced myself that they would acclaim me."

"The way," Gillian commented, "to make a dark object look pale is to place a darker object beside it. No, I don't think you have gauged your public as well as you generally do. Public opinion must not be set off with a hair-trigger. And how about your daughter?"

"I have convinced myself that Dorothy would not suffer."

"That," said Gillian, "is a splendid specimen of what my grandmother used to call wishful thinking. Dorothy would automatically be branded the daughter of a murderer, an ex-convict. You must not spoil her life."

"Then," Henshaw barked, "I have no choice but suicide."

"Leave the matter in my hands."

"What can you do? Robard demands an answer in forty-eight hours."

"He shall have an answer in forty-eight hours."

HENSHAW STARTED TO speak, but closed his mouth as the front door opened. A slim, pretty blond girl in summer sports costume came running into the living room. She was hatless. Her face was flushed and her eyes were starry. Behind her came a blushing young man.

Gillian said cordially: "Why! Hello, there, Dorothy!" And he nodded to the young man. He knew Dan Thompson only by reputation: the youngest son of one of the finest old families in Greenboro; a famous football player; a clear-eyed, clean-looking young man; the kind that Gillian especially admired. He would like to have a son just like Dan Thompson.

Dorothy had thrown herself on her father's lap. She was shaking his tawny head between her hands and expostulating:

"Dad, you said you wouldn't be longer than half an hour. We've been sitting in that car at least an hour and a half. But it's an ill wind that doesn't blow somebody somewhere—or however it runs. Dan, you tell him. Make your little speech, darling."

Dan Thompson blushed redder still. He gave Victor Henshaw a bashful, boyish smile. But he looked him squarely in the eye.

"Well, sir, you see—" he began and stopped. "We—we've been talking things over. I've got a good job and good prospects—and Dorothy and I want to get married."

The young man's chin was up now, and his shoulders were back. Victor Henshaw looked at him fiercely for a moment, then smiled.

"I feel honored, Dan, to be let into the secret. Most fathers nowadays are generally not informed until they receive an invitation to the wedding."

He shook Dan Thompson's hand and gravely kissed his daughter. He said to her:

"Run along, honey. I'll follow in ten seconds."

When the young man and the girl were gone, Gillian said:

"It would be a shame to bust that up."

"It won't be busted up if you can find some way of dealing with Don Robard," the publisher retorted desperately. "You're a smart man. It's my opinion that you're the smartest criminal lawyer in this State. You're as clever sometimes as the devil himself. But I suppose this affair of Vee-Anne's with Robard has stunned you—numbed your intellect."

Gillian said nothing. Henshaw went on:

"Look here. Have you been so blind? Haven't you been aware that this has been going on?"

"No," Gillian growled.

His friend snorted. "That's what love does to an otherwise smart man. You're the only member of the country club who hasn't noticed it. It's been going on for weeks, Gillian. Everybody is talking about it. They've been seen slipping off together in his car. She's been seen slipping out of his apartment. Where have your eyes been, man?"

Gillian made no answer. His friend continued:

"Until this afternoon, when we heard what we heard in the locker room, I thought you were being foxy. I thought you were planning to come down on him like a steam roller."

"I am planning it now."

"A great many husbands in this town will be grateful if you wipe him off the face of the earth."

"I will attend to him," said Gillian.

"And kill two birds with one stone?"

"I will attend to him," Gillian repeated.

"What are you planning to do?"

Gillian shrugged, but made no reply. The front door had opened again. This time it was Vee-Anne. She was pale. Her eyes looked dead. She paused in the doorway, and the glance she cast in at the two men was furtive. She murmured:

"I have a splitting headache, Gillian. I'm going straight to bed."

Neither of the men spoke until she was gone. Then Henshaw said in a low voice:

"Some husband will kill Robard if you don't."

"Yes," said Gillian. He accompanied the newspaper publisher to the veranda steps and waited until Victor Henshaw had entered his sedan. Then he reentered the house and went up to his study.

3

GRIM BUSINESS

GILLIAN HEARD VEE-ANNE moving about in their bedroom, but he did not call to her. From one of the desk drawers he removed a small automatic pistol. He went downstairs again and let himself quietly out of the house. He would not drive. He would walk. It was a half hour's walk to the Herrendon Arms and the night was cool. But in that half hour Gillian's blood did not grow cooler by a single degree. There was murder in his brain, in his heart, and in the hand that clutched the pistol in his coat pocket.

He would go up to Don Robard's apartment, unannounced. He would enter the apartment and he would say to Don Robard:

"I am going to kill you as I would kill a poisonous reptile."

Then he would shoot him through the heart.

Gillian adhered to this reckless plan until he saw the tall apartment building, sparkling with lights, looming ahead of him. Then it occurred to him that nothing he could do would give his enemies greater satisfaction than his killing of Don Robard. He could see the sensational headlines in the tabloids:

HAZELTINE SLAYS MAN WHO STOLE WIFE!

And he could see the smirk of delight on the face of Adelbert Yistle, the district attorney. How Bert Yistle, his adversary of many a legal battle, would love this opportunity of sending him to the electric chair!

There must be, Gillian reasoned, some other, some much more effective method of dealing with Don Robard.

Until dawn, Gillian walked the streets, turning over in his mind this scheme and that; always, in the end, discarding it. When the sun came up he was standing on a coal dock above the Sangamo River. Across the street was a building which Gillian knew well—a low brick building, shabby and forlorn. It was the city morgue.

Gillian frowned at it for some minutes, then slowly walked over. Asleep in a chair in the small office was an old man who snored. Gillian shook him by the shoulder and the old man jumped up, grinning.

"Mr. Hazeltine!" he wheezed. "Sure, and what are you doin' up at this hour of the night?"

"Mike," said Gillian, "you are a discreet man. Have you hauled anybody out of the river lately?"

"Yes, sir—not five hours ago, we hauled out a fine specimen of a man. A poor divil, Mr. Hazeltine, struck down by a bullet in the prime of his life. The police boat pulled him in about an hour after he was shot. And nobody will ever know who fired that shot, Mr. Hazeltine; because he was a poor, starvin' bootlegger who was in wrong with the gang. A nice, fine fellow he was, too."

"Do you know his name?"

"It was Herman Ochas, Mr. Hazeltine."

"What time was he shot?"

"A minute or two before or after midnight. Mr. Hazel-tine."

"And no one knows who shot him and threw him in the river?"

"No, sir; and no one ever will. Would you like to have a look at the poor fellow, Mr. Hazeltine?"

Gillian shuddered. In spite of his long years of association with murderers, he had never overcome an aversion to the sight of death. He hated dead men. Dead men terrified him.

"No," he said. "No, Mike." And hastened away from the place.

Gillian did not return to his home for breakfast, but ate leisurely and thoughtfully in a downtown restaurant. Immediately after breakfast he repaired to his office and telephoned police headquarters. He was presently Connected with Bill Murdock of the Homicide Squad.

"Who," Gillian asked Bill Murdock, "killed Herman Ochas, the bootlegger?"

"Who," the detective retorted affably, "killed Cock Robin? Nobody knows and nobody ever will and no one cares. Ochas was trying to horn into the liquor ring's business, and somebody decided that the time had come to take him for a ride."

"What do you know about the murder?"

"All I know is that 'assailant or assailants unknown' plugged him on the old salt dock and kicked him into the water. Some one heard the shot and the splash and called headquarters. A police boat found Ochas lodged between two of the piles, hooked him out and turned him over to the morgue. He had no kith or kin and will probably end up in potter's field."

THE SILVER FOX thanked him for his information and hung up. He was looking through the telephone directory for Don Robard's number when the phone rang. Victor Henshaw's harsh voice came down the line.

"Gillian? Where in the devil have you been all night? I've been trying to reach you at your house since half past twelve."

"What's wrong?" Gillian asked.

"Robard came to my house not five minutes after I'd reached home, after leaving you. We had it out hot and heavy until after twelve. He insists that if I don't come through with that half interest by six to-night—that's the deadline—he's going to every newspaper in town and tell what he knows. What am I going to do?"

"By six o'clock to-night," Gillian answered, "he'll have his mind on other matters. But let me get this straight, Vic. When Robard came to your house, who let him in?"

"He didn't come in. I was sitting on the front veranda, smoking and thinking things over—"

"Alone?"

"Yes, alone. He came up the walk and I met him. Why?"

"It's important, Vic. Did any one else see or hear the two of you talking out there?"

"Not a soul. The servants had retired. Dorothy and Dan dropped me off at the house and went on to the dance at the club. They didn't get back until after two. I was still sitting on the porch."

"I want to make sure of this," said Gillian. "No one, so far as you know, saw Robard come; no one but you saw him while he was there on the porch with you, and no one saw him go."

"That's so, Gillian, but what does it matter?"

"Victor," said Gillian, "are your affairs in order, so that, if I want you to, you can disappear at a moment's notice for a week or a month or even longer?"

"If it's necessary, I can do that."

"Have lunch with me," Gillian said, "and we'll go over certain details. Good-by."

He hung up, finished his search for Don Robard's number in the telephone directory, and called it. A manservant answered. When Don Robard's deep, rich, musical voice came over the wire, Gillian pitched his voice very low and said:

"Mr. Robard, this is police headquarters. Will you kindly tell me where you were last night between the hours of ten and one?"

There was a long pause. Then: "I was in bed. Why? What's the matter?"

"Can you produce any one to prove that you did not leave your apartment between the hours of ten and one?"

"If I can't," Robard snapped, "what of it?"

"Your servant wasn't there?"

"No. My servant goes home every night and comes here in the morning."

"You were absolutely alone?"

"I said I was! But look here. Who in the devil—"

Gillian hung up his receiver. He wore a grim smile.

4

AN ENEMY TO THE RESCUE

SHORTLY AFTER FIVE o'clock that afternoon, after one of the busiest days Gillian had ever spent, the door of his private office burst open and Vee-Anne came rushing in. Her eyes were dark with excitement. She was pale. She clutched the edge of Gillian's desk and got out in a thick, shaking voice:

"Gillian! They've arrested Don Robard and charged him with murdering a man!"

Gillian looked up into her tense white face. He felt sorry for Vee-Anne, but he felt much sorrier for Victor Henshaw and for himself.

"When did this happen, dear?"

"About an hour ago, Gillian. Two detectives came out to the country club and, without a word, put handcuffs on him and took him away in a sedan. Stanley Harvester asked them what Don had done, and they said he was wanted for murder. So I—I followed the sedan to the Fifth Precinct jail and—and they let me talk to him. Gillian!" She bent close to him, and her eyes upon him were those of a desperate woman, a stranger. "You must go down there and do what you can for him! It's a trumped-up charge—a frame-up! Don begged and implored me to have you go

29

down and see him. He knows how clever you are. Will you help him, darling?"

Gillian winced at that "darling." That Vee-Anne had tired of him and was in love with Don Robard was painful enough without this hypocrisy. But his stubborn pride would not permit him to denounce her. He would continue to treat her as he had always treated her. He wanted to shout: "Don't you think this is rubbing it in—asking me to help your damned lover?" But instead of that he said, gravely:

"What is there for me to do, Vee-Anne? A man charged with murder is not eligible, under the law, to bail. The law must simply take its course. I don't know Don Robard well. If he is innocent, he will be freed."

"But, Gillian, I tell you, it's a frame-up."

"And you want me to go down and have a talk with him."

"*He* wants you to go down. He knows how clever you are—"

"Yes, Vee-Anne; you said that before. I'll go down. I'll talk to him."

She straightened up with such obvious relief that Gillian's eyes involuntarily narrowed. His own wife begging him to save her lover from disgrace! Well, he was sorry for Vee-Anne; sorry that it was necessary to hurt her so. But he was a little resentful when, as they left the office, she clung to his arm and squeezed it and dabbled at her eyes with a little scented handkerchief. He wondered, as so many men have wondered before him, if it pays a man to be square and decent and honorable with women, when women, in return, seem so often to prefer scamps, rogues and even downright crooks. But he did not blame Vee-Anne. He blamed Don Robard. He hated Don Robard as he had never hated a man in his life. Gillian reflected: "In time, I'll probably forgive her. I love her so damned much I'd probably forgive her anything. But it will never be the same. The old feeling of security will be gone."

Vee-Anne drove him to the Fifth Precinct jail in the roadster he had given her for her birthday. He studied her profile as she maneuvered the car through traffic. And Gillian's heart grew heavier. He had never really fallen in love until he had met Vee-Anne. She was the prettiest and the cleverest woman he had ever known. And she had given him the happiest years of his life.

When she had stopped the car before the long flight of stone steps which led into the dingy red brick building, Vee-Anne said:

"Gillian, will you kiss me? You seem so strange."

Gillian kissed her, and the words echoed in his brain as his footfalls echoed in the jail corridor. So strange! So strange!

A WARDEN CONDUCTED him to Don Robard's cell. And Gillian knew something of the sweetness of revenge when he stopped before the cell and looked at the haggard face of his enemy. The golden bronze of the man's face was replaced by a mask of unhealthy gray. The liquid brown eyes stared out of the deep dark sockets. They were hypnotic, those eyes. No wonder women became infatuated with this man!

Don Robard clung to the lattice work of the cell door, and burst out in his rich, melodious voice:

"Gillian, did Vee-Anne tell you?"

"She told me that you had been arrested on a charge of murder."

"It's a frame-up!" Robard cried. "I knew this morning that something was cooking. Shortly before nine o'clock, some one telephoned my apartment—said they were phoning from police headquarters—wanted to know where I was last night between the hours of ten and one. I find that between those hours a bootlegger by the name of Herman Ochas was shot and thrown into the river. They're hanging that murder on me!"

Gillian said soothingly: "Don't worry, Don. All you have to do is establish an alibi. Where were you last night between ten and one?"

"I was home in bed."

"Well, then, produce witnesses to prove that you were home in bed at those hours and we'll squash this case against you in homicide court to-morrow morning."

"But I can't prove it," Robard protested. "My servant goes home at eight. He doesn't return until seven in the morning."

Sweat was standing out on the blackmailer's forehead and on his cheeks. Gillian watched a number of great drops start sliding down; saw them collect other drops and slide down Robard's face in a little forking river. He had been certain that Robard would not dare use Victor Henshaw for an alibi witness.

Robard burst out: "I tell you, Gillian, it's a frame-up."

"Who," Gillian inquired, "would frame you, Don?"

"The police."

Gillian frowned. He said: "I don't understand."

"Well, I'll tell you," said Robard, angrily. "As long as you are going to represent me, I may as well come clean."

"That," Gillian softly agreed, "is always wise. Never hold out on your lawyer."

"The truth is," Robard explained, "I've been putting some money into certain bootlegging operations. About six months ago, I learned where there was a certain large supply of Gordon gin and Scotch. It was a cache. The owners were afraid to move it."

"Where did you learn about it?" Gillian interrupted.

"From the chief of police." Robard looked at him and smiled a crooked smile. "I don't have to tell you about the ethics of bootlegging, Gillian. Every man is fair prey. Booze is booze. The chief of police was organizing a pool to buy that stock of liquor. He invited me into it. I beat him to it by buying up the cache myself. I sold it F.O.B. cache to a Cleveland liquor syndicate."

Gillian said to himself: "This rat would snatch the bread out of the mouth of his starving mother." Aloud: "And you think the chief of police, in revenge, has hung this murder on you?"

"I'm positive of it! He said he'd get me. He has got me! And there isn't a lawyer in America clever enough to wiggle me out of this jam but you, Gillian. I know that. I'm willing to pay you handsomely. Will you handle my case?"

"If one thing irritates me more than any other thing," was Gillian's answer, "it is to see a man charged with a murder that he did not commit. Of course I will help you, Don. But let me ask you a blunt question. A client must always come clean with his lawyer. Did you kill Herman Ochas?"

"Certainly not!" said the blackmailer, indignantly.

"**HAVE YOU A** criminal record, Don?"

"No! I was never arrested before in my life."

"Very well. I think we can enter court with our chins up and our heads back. We know you are innocent. We know that your past is spotless. We will defy the State to send you to the electric chair!"

Don Robard went paler still at that, as Gillian had known he would. He clutched the lattice work of the cell door and he blurted:

"Gillian, you mustn't let this go as far, even, as the grand jury. If you do, my reputation will be ruined! If I have to stand trial for murder—"

"We will try to avoid that," Gillian said consolingly. "You mustn't be afraid, Don."

"But you don't realize what a blow this is, Gillian," Robard burst out. "I've lived a clean, decent, upright life. And to have this outrageous charge hung on me—"

"If," Gillian interrupted, "you could only produce one good alibi witness—some man of unquestioned integrity—it would be so easy, so simple."

He watched the effect of that upon Don Robard. He saw the blackmailer's eyes go thoughtful. And he knew that Don Robard was thinking of Victor Henshaw, of what a perfect alibi witness the newspaper publisher would make. And he dared not ask Victor Henshaw to testify for him!

If he said to Victor Henshaw: "Please tell them where I was between the hours of ten and one last night! If you'll do that, I'll never blackmail you again!"—if he said that to Victor Henshaw, the publisher would not believe him. And if he threatened to expose Henshaw, Robard was fairly certain that Henshaw would tell him to do so—and go to the devil. On the horns of a dilemma was Don Robard, and Gillian watched his suffering with a certain secret enjoyment. He knew that Robard was asking himself: "Who would believe the word of a man accused of murder against the word of a man like Victor Henshaw?"

"No," Robard muttered. "I can produce no alibi witness. That is why I need you, Gillian. With your cleverness, it should not be difficult. Spend all the money you wish, bribing witnesses. Money is no object. We'll fight them with their own weapons! Why not buy an alibi witness?"

Gillian smothered an impulse to exclaim that a jail was too clean, too respectable a place for such a rat; and said instead: "Take things easy, Don. I must go back to the office now. I'll be on hand in homicide court in the morning when you're arraigned. Try not to worry. They're going to do their best to railroad you through to the electric chair, but if it is humanly possible to save you, I will."

"Good God!" Robard cried. "Do you really think there is a chance that they'll send me to the chair?"

"We will hope for the best," Gillian gravely answered, "and prepare for the worst."

He carried away with him a not unsatisfying picture of those hypnotic eyes glazed over by sudden panic. Don Robard was a thoroughly scared man; and by the time Gillian was through with him, he would be still more scared.

Gillian stepped into a public phone booth in the jail entrance and called Victor Henshaw at his house.

The newspaper publisher answered the phone. His voice was relieved, exultant. "I understand they've arrested Robard."

"Yes," said Gillian. "I've just talked to him. And the only possible alibi witness he can call, Victor, is leaving Greenboro to-night for points unknown to the authorities and for an indefinite stay. Are you packed?"

"Yes. I can leave on the eight-forty."

"Leave on it, Vic. Stay under cover. When I need you, I'll wire. Have a good rest. Good-by!"

GILLIAN LEFT THE jail and started down the steps. Two men were coming up. One of them he recognized as Josh Hammersley, who was a reporter on the *Times* and an old friend of Gillian's. The other was Mr. Adelbert Yistle, the district attorney.

Josh Hammersley wore a frown, but Mr. Yistle was grinning.

Josh said: "Gillian, what's the dope on this Robard business? It smells funny to me."

"It is funny," said Gillian. "The man is as innocent as a lamb."

The district attorney chuckled and said: "Isn't it wonderful the way Gillian rallies to the defense of the innocent lambs—even when they're smeared an inch thick with blood! You know damned well, Gillian, that Don Robard has the same moral principles as a fox in a henhouse. What I haven't been finding out about that skunk! He's been responsible for at least two family smash-ups."

"You can't send a man to the chair," Gillian argued, "because he's a philanderer."

"No," Mr. Yistle easily agreed. "I'm not going to send him to the chair because he's a philanderer. I'm going to send him to the chair because he's a deliberate, cold-blooded murderer. And as soon as I heard the rumor that you were going to defend him, I came hot-footing it right down. I don't get you at all, Gillian."

"You seldom do," Gillian murmured.

But the district attorney continued to gaze kindly at him.

"No, Gillian, I mean it. We've been enemies for a good many years. You've taken cases into court that I thought smelled to high heaven. A number of times you've convinced me—and a jury—that your clients were inno-cent. Mostly, it seems to me, your clients have been pretty decent people. They've been underdogs. They've appealed to the sympathy. They've had bad breaks. But this Robard—Gillian, I should think you'd be ashamed of yourself. He's a snake. I'm surprised that you don't volunteer to take over the prosecution. What possible extenuation can you have?"

"I think he's innocent."

"Bosh! Innocent or guilty, he's rotten. And I've heard some mean stories to-day, and I'm going to call a spade a spade, Gillian. People are saying that Don Robard and your wife—"

"Adelbert," said Gillian grimly, "if you mention my wife and Robard in public, in or out of a court room, every-thing else is going to stop while I pound your face in. I mean that."

Mr. Yistle's eyes narrowed. A wave of color flooded his square, massive face.

"I think we understand each other perfectly, Gillian. And I think your brain has gone soft. Robard is guilty as hell. I consider it my official duty and my personal duty to send that rascal to the chair."

"Circumstantial evidence!" Gillian scoffed.

"Eye witnesses!" snapped Mr. Yistle. "And I'll defy you to bulldoze them! Never have I had better witnesses!"

"This promises," put in the reporter, briskly rubbing his hands, "to be a nice, sensational trial."

"Have you ever," Gillian dryly inquired, "reported a trial in which Bert Yistle and I participated that wasn't sensational?"

ON THE FOLLOWING morning Don Robard was arraigned in the Homicide Court of Greenboro, charged with having planned and carried out the murder of Herman Ochas, motive or motives unknown. He was held without bail on a short affidavit for a hearing before the grand jury which was then sitting. And three days later, Don Robard appeared before the grand jury and pleaded not guilty. The grand jury, acting automatically, remanded the case to the superior court of Greenboro. Gillian and Mr. Yistle, independent of each other, pulled wires, and the newspaper-reading public was delighted to learn that "the Country Club Sheik" was to be tried immediately.

Don Robard, in the few weeks which elapsed between his arrest and his appearance in the court room, was seized upon hungrily by the tabloids. Here was a rare romantic figure! A prominent society man, a polo player, accused of murdering a common bootlegger! The tabloids intimated that his "love life" had been rich and full of variety. He was called a Don Juan, a Lothario and "a smoldering-eyed lady killer."

Gillian saw to it that his client was furnished with all these vivid newspaper descriptions. They infuriated Robard. He would glance at a photograph of himself on the front page of a peach-colored tabloid, and he would read the caption under it: "Rumored that Bootleg Murderer Was About to Establish a Love Cult. See page 3." Or: "Don Juan Robard's Trial Starts To-morrow. Court Room to be Packed with Love-Mad Women. Story on page 5." And Robard would throw the paper to the floor of his cell and curse.

"There must be some way of avoiding this beastly publicity."

"You will be lucky, Don, if you don't go to the chair."

"They can't have a case against me."

"These frame-ups are sometimes convincing."

"But you'll show them, Gillian! You've got to show them. You've got to go into that court room and make them realize how innocent I am! Why! I wouldn't hurt a—a kitten! You've got to make them see that. But I'm not afraid. No—I'm not afraid."

Perhaps he was not afraid, but he was certainly a changed man. The debonair Robard had become a morose, a snarling Robard. Gillian's contempt of him grew. And with it grew his hatred of the man. There were times when Gillian contemplated the picture of Don Robard strapped in the electric chair with actual pleasure. He knew that Don Robard was fighting against the strongest element in his nature—cowardice. Don Robard was yellow. But not until that yellow streak had showed itself would Gillian's plan be complete.

"You must not be too certain," he said. "After all, I'm nothing but a lawyer. I don't do anything supernatural in court rooms. Don't forget that a jury of twelve impartial men and women must decide on your guilt or innocence. The State has a strong case against you, Robard. Mr. Yistle is politically ambitious. To send you to the chair would be a feather in his cap."

"You won't let him send me to the chair, Gillian!" Robard's voice rang with confidence and assurance.

"If," Gillian said ruefully, "you could only provide me with one good, reliable alibi witness!"

At that, Robard became silent. The only alibi witness he might call to his defense, he dared not call.

ON THE NIGHT before the trial opened, Vee-Anne asked Gillian, over the dinner table, what Don Robard's chances were for an acquittal.

"It all depends on a certain witness."

Vee-Anne bent forward and looked under the candle flames at him.

"Who is this witness?"

"I'm afraid I can't say."

He had not meant to be so curt. He had tried, since that afternoon in the locker room, to act as if everything between them was the same. Now came a typical passage at arms.

"Gillian, you used to talk everything over with me. Why are you so mysterious about this case?"

"I didn't realize I'd been mysterious."

"You've been acting so—so differently lately. Has something happened? Don't you feel well? Are you angry at me about anything?"

"Have you done anything," Gillian answered, "that I should be angry about?"

She evaded a direct answer: "You've seemed so moody."

"I'm sorry. I didn't mean to be rude."

How long, Gillian wondered, could this farce continue?

She was pretending that she did not understand his mood-
iness, his strangeness. She was pretending that everything
between them was the same. And so was he. One of them
must, sooner or later, crack under the strain. Would it be
Vee-Anne or himself? He would say nothing until after
the trial. The outcome of the trial would point the way to
a great many things.

Vee-Anne was bending forward again. Her eyes, lumi-
nous in the candlelight, were looking up, searching his
face. Her hair gleamed like new copper. Her mouth was
red and soft.

"Gillian, I want you to tell me that you love me. You
haven't told me that in ages."

"Of course I love you."

"And you know that I love you, don't you, Gillian?"

"Yes, dear—of course!"

Gillian wanted to smash both fists down on the table.
What was her game? Why didn't she tell him outright that
she was tired of him, that she was living in the same house
with him only until he had somehow cleared her lover of
the charge hanging over him?

He asked himself: "Why am I so damned civilized? Why
don't I tell her what I think of this damned hypocrisy? Why
didn't I go up there and kill him that night?"

It occurred to him that at the hour when he was about to
go up to Robard's apartment and shoot him, Robard had
been sitting on Victor Henshaw's veranda.

Gillian smiled grimly. Some day soon, Robard would
crack. Some day soon, that streak of yellow would be
shown!

5

ON TRIAL FOR HIS LIFE

THE COURT ROOM was crowded to the doors. It was a hot Indian summer morning, and the air was stuffy and dense. The trial was about to begin. After two days of quarreling, of challenges, the jury was impanelled.

Judge Helman came in. Judge Helman was a sad-looking man of forty-eight or fifty with a pale, deeply lined face and dark, melancholy eyes. He had always reminded Gillian of Hamlet. His dignity was funereal. But he was one of the smartest judges on the bench. And he dealt harshly with perjury.

Every one remained standing until Judge Helman was seated.

Then a bailiff announced that court was open, and the judge said in his deep, unhappy voice: "You may call the jury."

The jury, seven men and five women, filed in presently, answered to their names, and were sworn. But no one in the court room was paying the slightest attention to the jury. Every eye was focused upon the dark, handsome man who sat at the counsels' table beside Gillian Hazeltine. Thanks to the enterprising tabloids, Don Robard had become, in the public's imagination, a sort of Bluebeard. He was handsomer than any one had expected; bronze-skinned, curly, dark hair, enormous dark eyes in great dark sockets—a man of romance and mystery. A sinister man. Women gazed at him and sighed.

Don Robard wore a gray tweed suit, and it made him look what he for years professed to be: an athlete, a sports-man, a gentleman.

Mr. Yistle, in a fiery voice, was addressing the jury.

"—and I will endeavor to prove to you, ladies and gentle-men of the jury, that, while this man—this society man, entered this court room presumably innocent, there is blood upon his hands. The blood of a poor wretch who chanced to cross his path and defied his will. I will prove to you that this Don Robard, who looks so much like a gentleman, is at heart the blackest of villains. I will prove to you that with the coldest deliberation, he took the life of Herman Ochas. My first witness is Dr. Bartrom."

Dr. Bartrom was the coroner of Greenboro. The white-haired old man made his way to the witness stand. His testimony was uninteresting but important.

It was necessary to establish the fact, for purposes of legal record, that there had been a Herman Ochas, and that Herman Ochas had come to his death by violent means.

The coroner testified that he had known Herman Ochas by sight; that on the night of September 16, he had been called to the morgue to examine the corpse of a man which had been taken out of the river by the police.

"How, in your opinion, Dr. Bartrom, was the death of Heiman Ochas brought about?"

Dr. Bartrom answered: "A .38 caliber revolver bullet caused his death. The bullet entered the left side between the fourth and fifth ribs, pierced the pericardium, and traversed the heart, causing almost instantaneous death."

"Did you probe for the bullet?"

"Yes, sir."

"Did you find it?"

"No, sir."

"That will be all, doctor. Does the defense wish to cross-examine?"

Gillian waved his hand in dismissal. The next witness was a pale-faced man with striking blue eyes and a black toothbrush mustache. He took the stand with an air of confidence and stated that his name was Charles Murchison.

MR. YISTLE: "WHAT is your occupation or business?"

"I run a restaurant on River Street."

"A hot dog stand, isn't it?"

"Yes, sir; you might call it that. But I don't specialize in hot dogs. I serve about every kind of food a hungry man would want."

"Is your restaurant open for business all night?"

"Yes, sir; day and night. My brother Jim runs it in the daytime, and I do the night trick."

"Were you, Mr. Murchison, behind the counter of your restaurant on the night of September 16?"

"I was. Yes, sir. From six at night until six the next morning."

"Mr. Murchison, I want you to look carefully at the man seated at the table over there—the man in the gray suit. Look at that man carefully, Mr. Murchison, and tell the ladies and gentlemen of the jury if you have ever seen him before."

"Yes, sir. I recognize him."

"Did you see him on the night of September 16 in your restaurant?"

"Yes, sir. Him and another fellow."

"What time did he and the other fellow enter your restaurant?"

"About ten o'clock, I should say."

Don Robard twisted his handsome head and whispered into Gillian's ear: "Are you going to let him get away with that? He never saw me before in his life!"

"What can we do?" Gillian answered.

"You can say he's a damned liar!"

"But how can we prove it?"

Gillian saw that tiny beads of perspiration had formed on his client's handsome forehead. Well, the court room was hot.

Mr. Yistle barked: "Who was that other fellow?"

And the witness clearly answered: "Herman Ochas, sir."

"How did you know the other man was Herman Ochas?"

"Because I knew the poor fellow well, sir. We were close friends, you might say. He used to drop in for most of his meals."

"Do you know what Herman Ochas's occupation was?"

"Yes, sir," the witness answered in a low voice. "He was a bootlegger."

Mr. Yistle rubbed his hands briskly. He cast a sharp glance at Gillian; a somewhat inquiring glance. In fact, there was an element of surprise in Mr. Yistle's glance. Ordinarily, Gillian would never permit testimony to follow so straight a line. Ordinarily. Gillian was constantly interrupting with objections. But Gillian sat, relaxed, in his chair, dreamily looking at the witness.

"Now, Mr. Murchison," said Mr. Yistle, "I want you to tell the jury in your own words what happened in your restaurant at about ten o'clock on the night of September 16."

The hot dog stand proprietor dutifully shifted his blue-eyed gaze to the jury.

"I was alone in my restaurant at about ten o'clock," he said, "when the door opened and in came that gentleman sitting over there. Right behind him was my poor old friend Herman Ochas. This gentleman—this Mr. Robard—came in and sat down on a stool at the counter and said he wanted a cup of coffee. Herman came and sat down on the stool beside him. He wanted an order of coffee and doughnuts. So I drew the coffee for the two gents and served Herman his doughnuts. Then I went and sat down on a chair at the end of the counter."

The witness paused. Don Robard was clutching Gillian's arm.

"How," he whispered, "can you convince the jury that all this isn't a pack of lies? Can't you get up and object?"

"On what grounds," Gillian answered, "shall I object?"

"On any grounds! I don't care!"

"So far," said Gillian, "every question and every answer has been absolutely legal. The objection would be overruled by the judge. Don't worry, Don."

"But can't you see that they are forging a chain of damnable lies that will drag me to the chair unless you do something to prevent them?"

"They haven't forged it yet," Gillian argued. "Don, if you

"You're letting them send me to the chair!"

could only produce some absolutely unimpeachable alibi witness—how easy it would be! We would spike their guns in a hurry."

THE WITNESS, WHO had just identified Robard as the man who had been in his hot-dog stand with Ochas just before the murder, was saying: "Of course, it's none o' my business listening to the talk that goes on between two of my customers. I'm not that kind. But there wasn't anybody else in my restaurant, and they talked so loud I couldn't help hearing. Must I tell what they were saying?"

"You have sworn," Mr. Yistle answered, "to tell the truth and the whole truth. Proceed, Mr. Murchison."

Mr. Murchison sighed and continued.

"Well, they began talkin' about some deal they had on to sell a lot of liquor. Mr. Robard over there had bought a lot of liquor from some prohibition agents who had confiscated it in a raid. And he had turned it over to poor old Herman Ochas. He wanted to know where the money from it was, and Herman said that he didn't have the money and he didn't have the liquor, because somebody found his cache and had stolen all the liquor."

Mr. Yistle interrupted: "Mr. Murchison, can you remember their exact words?"

"I can remember some of 'em. Mr. Robard said: 'Herman, I think you're a lying scoundrel and a sneak.' And Herman said: 'Mr. Robard, I wouldn't lie to any man. You ought to know, from your past experience, how crooked the men in this liquor racket, are.' Somebody got into that shed and got away with all that booze. And Mr. Robard kept saying that Herman was an out-and-out liar and a thief and a lot of other names that I can't mention with ladies present. And Herman kept protesting that he wasn't a liar or a thief."

"Did Herman Ochas lose his temper?"

"No, sir; he did not. Herman was always a quiet, peaceable man."

"Did the accused—Mr. Robard—lose his temper?"

"Yes, sir; he did. And I got pretty scared. He kept calling Herman a liar and a scoundrel and a crook and a river rat—every name he could lay his tongue to—and finally he said: 'You know, don't you, what happens in this business to men who double cross?' And Herman said: 'Please don't talk like that, Mr. Robard. I never double crossed you. That liquor was stolen out of that shed.' And when he said that, Mr. Robard jumped up, and there was a gun in his hand."

"A revolver or a pistol?"

"A revolver, it was—a big blue revolver. I just caught a glimpse of it, and then he shoved it right back into his pocket, as if he'd changed his mind about something."

Gillian was on his feet. "I object to that, your honor. It is assumption."

"Sustained," ruled Judge Helman.

Don Robard whispered fiercely: "My God, Gillian, is that all you're going to object to?"

"It's all I can legally object to."

"But don't you realize that every word he said is a lie? Don't you see that they're building up the most spurious kind of a case?"

"Of course I do. But nothing can be done about it."

"You mean to say," Robard panted, his eyes blazing into Gillian's, "that you're going to sit here like this while they bring on witness after witness to stuff that jury with their lies?"

"I am helpless," said Gillian.

"Well, I'm not." Don Robard jumped up. In his rich, deep, musical voice he cried: "Your honor, I object to this. That man is a liar. Every word he has uttered is a lie. He never saw me before he entered this court room. I was never in his restaurant—his hot-dog stand!"

A BAILIFF WAS banging with his gavel. The court room burst into humming conversation. The bailiff banged. Judge Helman gazed sternly at Don Robard.

"You are represented by competent counsel. Anything you wish to say to the jury or to this bench must be uttered through your counsel."

"But—"

"The State will proceed."

Don Robard, mopping his dark, handsome face, sat down and looked at Gillian dazedly. Then his eyes cleared. He whispered hoarsely:

"It's a frame-up. A cold-blooded frame-up! And I believe you're in it. I don't believe you're going to lift a hand to save me!"

"Calm yourself, Don," Gillian soothed him. "When the time comes, I will exert every effort to save you. But the time hasn't come. Don—if only you could produce an alibi witness!"

The blackmailer glared at him suspiciously a moment longer, then relapsed again into brooding silence.

Mr. Yistle, with silence restored, said: "You may go on, Mr. Murchison. You were saying that the accused produced a blue revolver, then returned it to his pocket. What happened then?"

"Well, sir, a sort of funny look came into his eyes. It was a sort of a calculating look. And he said, in a funny voice, 'Well, Herman, I guess nothing is to be gained by arguing. Let's take a walk down to that shed.' And Herman said, 'All right, Mr. Robard; I want you to be certain that I'm not a liar or a double crosser.'

"They went out," said Mr. Murchison, "and that was the last I ever saw of my old friend Herman. The next thing I knew, Mr. Robard had shot him with that revolver."

"I object to that!" Gillian barked. "Did the witness see the accused shoot Herman Ochas?"

"No, sir. I heard about it, though."

"Strike that from the record," ordered Judge Helman in his mournful voice.

Mr. Yistle was wearing a catlike smile. He had done very well with this witness.

"That will be all. Does my esteemed friend wish to take this witness?"

His esteemed friend did wish to cross-examine the witness. Gillian got up and walked over to within a yard of Mr. Murchison and gazed at him steadily for several seconds.

"Mr. Murchison, are you quite sure that the man who came into your restaurant at about ten o'clock on the night of September 16 was Mr. Robard?"

"Yes, sir," the witness defiantly answered; "I am dead certain."

"How are your eyes?"

"They are fine."

"How is the lighting in your restaurant?"

"It is a fine lighting system."

"And there is no doubt in your mind that Mr. Robard was the man who came into your restaurant that night with Herman Ochas?"

"I said I was sure, didn't I?"

"Mr. Murchison, were you ever arrested on a criminal charge?"

"No, sir; never," said the witness.

"That will be ail."

Judge Heiman said: "We will take a recess for lunch. The jury will retire."

6

DRAWING THE NOOSE

GILLIAN ACCOMPANIED DON Robard back to his cell. His client was in a nasty mood.

"I mean it," said Robard. "I'm suspicious of you. I don't think you have the slightest intention of trying to save me. I think you're part of the frame-up."

"Why," Gillian dryly inquired, "don't you change counsel? It's permissible, you know."

"Who would I get?"

"You might try Clarence Darrow, except that he's in Europe."

Don Robard was perspiring. He paced to and fro in his narrow cell. He suddenly turned and whipped out:

"Look here, Gillian; you haven't got anything against me, have you?"

Gillian gasped in convincing amazement "What could have put such a thought into your head?"

"I don't understand you!"

"Very few people do," admitted the Silver Fox.

"I'd certainly hate to have you against me. I know how you treat your enemies. I know that more than one man you hated was tickled to death to get out of this town with his life—and never come back."

"That," Gillian agreed, "has happened to some of my enemies. When I have it in for a man, he is usually sorry. Because I'm like an elephant, because I never forget or forgive a man who does me wrong or who does wrong to any one I'm fond of."

"But have I ever done any wrong to you?"

"If you have," said Gillian, "you would certainly know about it, wouldn't you?"

Don Robard was now sweating freely, and the heat of his cell was not entirely accountable. His eyes, for the first time, had a hunted look.

"Would you mind," he burst out, "if I changed lawyers?"

"Not at all, Don. Whom would you like to have?"

Don Robard clasped his hands and began again to pace. He stopped and said, in his deep, melodious voice:

"But if I retained a new lawyer, and if you had something against me, you'd still somehow get me."

"It seems to me," said Gillian, "that you are building up a hypothetical case. But if it were true—yes, I would still get you. If I wanted to get you, I would."

"But you're actually trying to save me."

"My sworn duty to every client is to try to save him. And how easily, Don, I could save you—if you hadn't been asleep on the night of September 16. If you had only been visiting some reputable and credible citizen of Greenboro!"

Don Robard stared at him a moment longer, then fell to rubbing his hands and pacing again.

A deputy sheriff came down the corridor and said: "The jury's in, Mr. Hazeltine."

Gillian had gone without lunch, but he did not regret it. Unless he was mistaken, Don Robard was beginning to weaken. It would not be long before he cracked. And Gillian wanted to see the streak of yellow which he knew dominated Robard's make-up.

THE STATE'S FIRST witness for the afternoon session was a brightfaced old Irishwoman who gave her name as Maggie O'Toole. She smiled pertly at the jury; she smiled pertly at Mr. Yistle, at the judge, at Gillian. Only upon Don Robard did she bestow an unfriendly glance. Her twinkling eyes became steady and dark. One corner of her generous mouth lifted up a little.

Robard whispered to Gillian, "What whopping lies is she going to tell?"

"We shall see," said Gillian.

"You aren't worried?"

"Not at all. Truth, Don, has a way of finding its path through the most intricate maze of lies."

But Don Robard looked unconvinced.

Mr. Yistle was questioning the witness: "What is your occupation?"

"You mean my job?" retorted the pert old Irishwoman. "I'm a scrub lady. I scrub floors. I empty wastebaskets and garboons in the Atchison Building."

"At what hour do you go to work?"

"I go to work at six so sharp that you could set a clock by me!"

The court room tittered. The bailiff brought his gavel down and glared.

"And at what hour do you stop working, Mrs. O'Toole?"

"At half past ten, sir."

"Then you go home?"

"I do, sir; yes, sir."

"Where do you live, Mrs. O'Toole?"

"In the boarding house that I run down by the gas tanks on River Street."

"You walk home?"

"Yes, sir. I'm a strong, healthy woman, sir."

"I'm sure we're glad to know that, Mrs. O'Toole. Now, I want you to tell the jury if anything interesting happened while you were walking home along River Street at about half past ten on the night of September 16."

"I was walkin' along River Street," responded Mrs. O'Toole, "mindin' me own business, as usual, when I saw two men comin' down the street toward me. They were walkin' along slow, and they were talkin' loud and fast. At least one of them was."

"Did you see those men's faces?"

"I did, sir. They were near a street light when we passed."

"Did you recognize either of them?"

"I recognized one of them, sir, as Herman Ochas, the bootlegger. He boarded with me, sir, and a nice, clean, good-natured man he was, sir. Always prompt to pay his room rent. Always with a cheery word for everybody. Always stoopin' down to pat some stray child or dog on the head, sir."

"It seems to me, your honor," Gillian interrupted, "that the witness is dealing in irrelevancies."

"The witness," ordered Judge Helman, "will confine herself to direct answers to questions."

"But I was answerin' the question direct, judge," protested Mrs. O'Toole. "He ast me did I reco'nize poor Herman Ochas, and all I said was yes!"

It was again necessary for the bailiff to use his gavel to stop the laughter. Mr. Yistle then resumed his examination. **"DID YOU RECOGNIZE** the man with whom Herman Ochas was walking?"

"Not at the time, sir. But I reco'nize him right now. It's that black scoundrel sittin' over there wit' murder for me in his eyes!"

Judge Helman turned to her impatiently. "I must ask you, again, Mrs. O'Toole, to answer questions directly. If you recognize the man, in this court room, whom you saw walking with Herman Ochas, you may indicate him and answer in the affirmative."

Maggie O'Toole indicated Don Robard by stretching out a long skinny arm and pointing an extremely red forefinger at him.

"There he sits, the rascal!"

Don Robard looked bored, uneasy and indignant.

Mr. Yistle promptly helped the witness. "That man sitting over there in the gray suit?"

"That's the rascal!"

"Gillian," Robard whispered huskily, "can't you do anything about that lying old hag?"

"Wait," Gillian counseled.

Mr. Yistle: "Mrs. O'Toole, you say you recognized Herman Ochas, and you say you can now identify this man, the accused, as his companion that night."

"I say it, and I say it again!"

"Very well. When you passed them, did you overhear any of their conversation?"

"Indeed, I did, sir. I heard enough to scare me half out of me shoes! I heard that rascal over there say: 'I won't tell

you again what happens in this business to double crossers!'
And as plain as the nose on my face, I heard poor Herman
Ochas say, 'But I haven't double crossed you, Mr. Robard.
Please don't shoot a man who hasn't done you any wrong.'"

Even the ladies and gentlemen of the jury were leaning
forward. The mouths of most of the spectators were ajar.
Don Robard was sitting stiffly upright, his jaw muscles
bulging, his eyes blazing at Maggie O'Toole. He turned
to Gillian.

"Do you mean to say," he demanded in a hoarse whisper,
"that you're going to let her get away with that?"

"What has she said," Gillian returned, "that I can legally
object to? Of course, she's lying. You know it. I know it."

"But the jury doesn't know it!"

"The jury will!"

"But how, man, how?"

"Wait," cautioned Gillian. "Our time will come."

And he gave the blackmailer a glance which might have
been likened to that of a wheeling hawk in the air, watching the struggles of a rabbit that has been caught in a trap.

The questions and answers continued. Said Mr. Yistle:

"Mrs. O'Toole, did you clearly hear Herman Ochas say:
'Please don't shoot a man who hasn't done you any wrong?'"

"Indeed I did, sir."

"Did you hear any more of their conversation?"

"Nothing as clear as that, sir. The rest I heard was just
broken-up words. Mr. Robard was cursing and swearing,
and Herman Ochas was pleadin' with him."

"When these two men passed on, what did you do, Mrs.
O'Toole?"

"I just stood there on the sidewalk, like I was frozen

to it—so scairt I was. And I watched them walk away. I watched 'em till they went around the corner into Polk Street."

"Which way did they turn?"

"T'ward the river, sir—t'ward the old salt dock."

"And you stood there, scared, did you, Mrs. O'Toole, until those two men were gone from sight toward the old salt dock?"

"I did, sir. I was too scared to move."

"And then what did you do?"

"I scampered along home, sir. And I waited up for Herman Ochas to come in. I waited till three o'clock in the mornin', and then I went up to his room and sat m'self down on the edge of his bed, and there I sat till the sun came up, waitin' and worryin' and wonderin'. But he never come home. All that time I was settin' on the edge of his bed, he was lyin' there, cold and stiff, in the morgue! And this rascal was makin' his getaway from the scene of his crime—the cold-blooded murderer!"

"Objection!" Gillian roared.

"Sustained. Strike that last sentence from the record."

"That will be all," stated Mr. Yistle.

"NOW, GET UP," prompted Don Robard frantically, "and tell her what a liar she is."

Gillian arose. He walked over to Mrs. O'Toole and smiled at her. The Irishwoman gave him a glance in return.

"Mrs. O'Toole," he said gently, "you came into this court room to-day to help us find the murderer of Herman Ochas, did you not?"

"I did that. And I hope I've done my little bit."

"Let us all hope so, Mrs. O'Toole. On the night of

September 16, when you were walking home from your employment and you overheard the conversation between Herman Ochas and the accused, may I ask if you had been drinking?"

The scrub lady glared at him.

"A nice, polite question that is to ask a decent, respectable, hard-working woman!"

"Will you answer it, Mrs. O'Toole?"

"Indeed I will answer it! I will answer more than that! I will say that not one drop of hard liquor has gone down this throat in twenty years! I am not a drinking woman, I'll have you understand! You and that rascal of yours!"

"Were you, Mrs. O'Toole, ever arrested on a criminal charge?"

"Your honor," Mr. Yistle interrupted, "I object to this line of questioning. I realize that the esteemed counsel for the defense is attempting to impeach the credibility of this witness. But I must object to the form his attempted impeachment is taking." Judge Helman looked mournfully at Mr. Yistle.

"I must overrule your objection, Mr. Yistle. Mr. Hazeltine has remained quite within his legal bounds. You may proceed, Mr. Hazeltine."

Gillian proceeded: "Will the witness answer my last question?"

"Indeed she will!" Mrs. O'Toole cried. "No! I was never arrested on any charge. I am a decent, respectable, law-abiding woman!"

"And on the witness stand just now, you have told the truth, the whole truth and nothing but the truth?"

"Oh, so I am a liar now, am I, as well as a drunkard and a criminal?"

"That will be all," said Gillian.

"It had better be all, and it seems to me that a good lawyer like you are could be spendin' his time better than to come into a court room to defend a scamp like that one over there!"

And Maggie O'Toole, to the regret of every one in the court room with the possible exception of the man accused of murder, descended from the witness stand.

THE DISTRICT ATTORNEY was gazing at Gillian with an air of puzzlement. His brows were knitted, and, there was a deep furrow between his eyes. Then his air of assurance returned, and he called, in a clear, firm voice, his next witness.

A gorilla of a man came lurching down the aisle and to the witness stand. But Gillian was not watching him; he was watching his client.

Don Robard's bronze complexion had turned gradually yellow. The look of the hunted animal was more and more perceptible in his eyes. The yellow streak, Gillian was certain, was beginning to reveal itself. The blackmailer would presently realize that he was crowded into a tight corner; that there was but one way of escape.

He whispered anxiously to Gillian: "Do you know if Victor Henshaw is in the court room?"

Gillian answered, with well-simulated surprise: "Why do you want to see Victor Henshaw?"

"I'd like to see him immediately after this session. It—it's an important business matter."

"Henshaw," said Gillian, "is out of the city."

He saw Robard go a shade paler. "How many more witnesses will these devils use?"

"Not many, Don. They seem to have you pretty well surrounded."

"But what are you going to do?"

"Wait."

"Look here! You are in on this frame-up! You're deliberately letting them send me to the chair! You've deliberately helped them get me into this corner! You want to see me electrocuted! Damn you, you helped them—"

"Steady!" warned Gillian.

Don Robard stared at him a moment longer, then subsided.

Gillian watched him. Robard was cracking. It would not be long.

The gorilla-like man had taken the witness stand. He had close set eyes. His blue-black hair came to a peak over his eyes. They were ugly eyes. He gave his name as Nick Whaley.

"Nicholas?"

"I said Nick." This was a growl; it was accompanied by a frown.

Nick Whaley was sworn. His occupation, he said in response to Mr. Yistle's first question, was night watchman. He was in the employ of the Ludlow Salt Works.

"Is it part of your duty, Mr. Whaley, to patrol the old salt dock at the foot of Polk Street?"

Nick Whaley folded his hairy red hands on his stomach and answered: "Yes." He gave Gillian a sultry glance.

Mr. Yistle: "Did you ever know a man by the name of Herman Ochas?"

"Yes; I knew him well."

"Did he not keep a small motor boat tied up beside the old salt dock?"

"He did," answered the gorilla man.

"And did he not make certain use of a small shed, or shanty, on the northeastern corner of the old salt dock?"

"Yes. It was an old tool shed. He used it to store parts of his motor boat when he wasn't using the boat—odds and ends of rope, anchors, and so forth."

"You let him use that shed, did you?"

NICK WHALEY DID not answer at once. He finally said: "I didn't stop him from usin' it. Nobody else was usin' it. He patched up the holes in the roof and used it, and nobody stopped him."

"I see. Do you know if Herman Ochas ever stored liquor in that shed?"

No."

"You mean, he didn't?"

"I mean, I don't know. He stowed stuff in the shed, and he took it away. He was a peaceable guy. He was friendly to me. I knew there wasn't nothin' on the old salt dock for him to steal. He came and went as he pleased. My job was to keep a lookout for fires. Herman Ochas was all right. He used to go my rounds with me sometimes. Night watchin' is a lonely job."

"Do you know if Herman Ochas ever used his motor boat for transporting liquor?"

"I don't know. It was none of my business."

Gillian interjected: "A night watchman might have made it his business."

The gorilla-like man gazed dully at him. "Well, I didn't make it my business."

Mr. Yistle: "Now, Mr. Whaley, I wish you would tell the jury in detail of the events you observed on the old salt dock about midnight on the night of September 16."

Mr. Whaley fixed his sultry gaze on the jury.

"Herman had a feller with him that night—that feller sittin' over there." He flung out a long arm unexpectedly at Don Robard, and the blackmailer stirred uneasily. He was so pale now that Gillian was beginning to wonder if he might not be on the verge of toppling out of his chair. Don Robard was clenching his hands between his knees. His lips were parted upon his fine white teeth, and his eyes were staring. They looked glassy.

Mr. Yistle snapped: "You mean Don Robard?"

"I do. Him and Herman were on the dock when I made my eleven o'clock rounds. Herman was showin' him around the shed, sort of explainin' things to him. I didn't hear what they were sayin'. It wasn't none of my business."

Mr. Yistle interrupted: "Is there a light down on the dock?"

"No; there ain't a light within a block of the dock."

"How did you recognize Herman Ochas and Mr. Robard?"

"I flashed my light on them. I held it on for mebbe ten seconds. Herman says: 'It's all right, Nick. This gentleman and I are just discussin' some business.' So I flashed off my light and went on about my own business. I didn't see 'em again until an hour later, when I made my twelve o'clock rounds. At first I didn't see nothin'. I come down Polk

Street and onto the inshore end of the dock, right by the shanty there. Then I heard their voices."

"Did you recognize them by their voices?"

"Sure, I did. I knew Herman's voice well, and this man's voice, this Don Robard, has a deep voice like a pipe organ in a movie theater. They were out on the end of the dock. I thought they were gettin' ready to climb down the ladder there into Herman's putt-putt. But they stood there talkin'. I heard Herman say, 'I wish I could make you see it my way, Mr. Robard. I ain't a crook and I ain't a double-crosser and I ain't a liar.' I knew right then that hell was poppin'. I knew that poor old Herman was in trouble. So I started hot-footin' it out to the end of the dock."

The witness paused. Certainly the most important, the most telling, witness so far, he had reduced the court room to a silence in which a man's asthmatic breathing, in the farthest corner, could be loudly heard.

DON ROBARD, GRAY now with his emotions, was gripping the arms of his chair and straining forward, as if, at another word, he would launch himself at the hairy man on the stand.

Nick Whaley went on:

"Just as I started t'ord the end of the dock, this Robard said, loud and clear: 'You won't double-cross anybody else, you lying sneak!' I didn't see him pull the gun, because it was so dark. But I saw the red flash of it, and I heard the bang of it. It sounded to me like the roar of a cannon. I started runnin' t'ord him, as I said, just when the gun went off. Next thing I knew, I had tripped up on the loose end of an old plank that had curled up with the heat and rain, and I went smackin' down on my face. It clean knocked the breath out of me. I guess I must o' laid down there, flat on my stomach, for pretty close to half a minute, tryin' to get my wind back. While I was layin' there, I heard a splash in the water, then this feller here, this Robard, came runnin' past me and up Polk Street. I watched him, on my hands and knees, pass under a street light on the corner there of Polk and River. And it was this feller all right. He had plugged Herman, kicked him into the drink, and run."

Nick Whaley paused. Don Robard, with his eyes fixed hypnotically on him, was half out of his chair, gripping the arms until his knuckles were white.

The witness went on: "I walked out to the end of the dock and flashed my light around, but there wasn't no sign of Herman. Then I got nervous. I ran back to the factory and called up the police."

Don Robard sprang to his feet, knocked his chair over and ran around the end of the counsel table. Gillian watched him with alert gray eyes. The moment he had been awaiting had come. Don Robard was cracking!

A sheriff sprang at Robard and grasped him by one arm. Robard struck him savagely in the face, and the sheriff seemed to wilt. Another sheriff leaped upon him, wrapped an arm about his neck and locked the hold with his other hand.

Robard shook his free fist at the man on the witness stand.

"You liar!" he shouted. "You dirty rotten liar!"

Nick Whaley had risen. There was an ugly grin on his lips. He bundled his huge hairy hands into fists at his side and waited. But the sheriff held on. The other one came unsteadily to his feet. Steel glinted. Handcuffs snapped upon the blackmailer's wrists.

The court room was in an uproar. A bailiff banged with his gavel. Gillian had arisen with a faint smile. Mr. Yistle, in a momentary lull, added his climax to the scene:

"Your honor, the State rests."

7

DETERMINED MEN

JUDGE HELMAN HAD arisen. He banged on his desk and said sternly: "Return the accused to his cell. If order cannot be restored in this court, I will order the room cleared. The defense may proceed."

Gillian stepped up to the bench. "Your honor," he said, "I shall require until to-morrow morning to finish the preparation of my case. It may be necessary for me to summon a witness who is out of the city. Will you permit me to open the defense in the morning?"

"It is granted," ruled Judge Helman. He turned to the jury.

"Ladies and gentlemen of the jury, we are about to take a recess until tomorrow morning at ten o'clock. The Court admonishes you not to speak about this case among yourselves or permit any one to speak to you about it. You will keep your minds open until the case is finally submitted to you."

Mr. Yistle seized Gillian by the arm. The district attorney wore a wide, exultant grin.

"Well, Gil, do you admit you're licked? Can you kick a hole in my case?"

"The holes in your case," Gillian answered, "are big enough for a Zeppelin to fly through."

"You mean, you think you can bring in a verdict for that rat after the testimony the jury has heard to-day?"

"That's what I intend to do, Adelbert."

Mr. Yistle threw back his head and laughed. It was loud, irritating laughter. Gillian watched the district attorney's merriment with a faint frown.

Judge Helman leaned over the bench toward them.

"If it's as funny as that," said the mournful judge, "let me in on it."

"It's funny enough, Jerry," chuckled Mr. Yistle. "Gil says he still has a case."

And for the first time to-day, Judge Helman smiled. It was an astonishing smile; it seemed to extend from one judicial ear to the other. The judge asked:

"What's your defense, Gil?"

"Alibi," said Gillian. He walked toward the jail with the laughter of Judge Helman and Mr. Yistle ringing in his ears.

Gillian found Don Robard clutching the bars of his cell door. His head moved from side to side like that of a caged, untamed animal. His lower lip was protruding. He snarled:

"You damned dirty louse, you've got me cooked!"

Gillian looked at him with round, innocent eyes.

"Don," he breathed, as if he were shocked, "aren't you using pretty harsh words?"

"You damned double-crosser! You took my case with the deliberate intention of railroading me to the chair! There isn't any possible way of saving me, and you know it!"

"That," Gillian murmured, "isn't quite true. There is a way

of saving you. Give me the name of some decent, reputable citizen with whom you spent the hours from ten to half past twelve on the night of September 16—and you'll be a free man by noon tomorrow."

Don Robard began to curse. He paced up and down in the narrow confines of his cell and he wrung his hands. From time to time he shot a murderous look at Gillian and cursed at him. Gillian stood and watched him with a mild but catlike curiosity. Don Robard was a rat in a trap. Only one man could save him from a hideous interlude which would end with his being strapped in that horrible piece of furniture known as the electric chair. And that man could be reached only through Gillian Hazeltine.

Gillian watched the sweat stream in small rivers down the lemon-colored face of the blackmailer.

DON ROBARD REACHED the far end of his cell. His step became suddenly uncertain. Gillian watched him sharply. He knew that Robard was on the very verge of collapse. The man pivoted about and came staggering to the door. His mouth was open, and he was breathing through it stertorously. His eyes were wild; they seemed to bulge. He panted:

"You've got me licked! I'll do anything you say! Get Victor Henshaw! I'll make any bargain you say! I'll do anything you tell me! But get Henshaw by to-morrow morning!"

"You spent the evening of September 16 with Victor Henshaw?" said Gillian.

"You know I did! Yes!"

"Blackmailing him for more money—a half interest in the *Times?*"

"Yes, yes. I'll do anything you say. I'll make any promise and I'll keep it! I want to get out of this town! I know you hate me! I know what you'll do to me if I ever come back. Oh, I know you now, Hazeltine! I'll never cross you again."

"No," said Gillian. "You'll never, cross me again."

"I'll never return to Greenboro!"

"Never," said Gillian.

"You'll get Henshaw to come to court and testify for me?"

"Yes," said Gillian.

He left the jail and walked to his office. A great load was removed from Gillian's shoulders. For the first time in weeks, he felt happy. Reaching his office in the Atchison Building, Gillian put in a long distance call for the hunting lodge on Lake Carmo where Victor Henshaw was in seclusion.

It was an excited, exultant Henshaw who answered his call.

"Gillian," he cried, "you've done wonders. I've had hourly reports on the trial radioed to me up here, and I want to tell you you've done a masterly job. That last witness, that night watchman, was superb. We've got that snake where we want him—at last!"

"Yes," Gillian agreed, "and he is willing to talk business. When can you leave for Greenboro?"

The newspaper publisher chuckled. "I've changed my mind. I'm not coming."

"You mean," Gillian gasped, "you won't testify for him?"

"That's just what I mean. Damn him, he's made me suffer for fifteen years. He's put white hairs in my head and he's carved lines in my face. You've got him beautifully trapped. Let him go to the chair! To-morrow morning, you can simply state that you have no defense. Robard will be dead in a month."

Gillian snapped: "You're out of your senses!"

"I am taking a well-earned revenge."

"Victor," Gillian said grimly, "you will catch the first train for Greenboro. You will be here by ten to-morrow morning."

"Try and make me! The only train from here which would reach Greenboro before ten to-morrow morning leaves in one hour. I'm going to miss that train. And I'll bet you a thousand dollars that Judge Helman will not grant you another postponement!"

GILLIAN JAMMED THE receiver down on its hook, got his hat, and raced out of his office. At the curb in front of the Atchison Building he hailed a cruising taxicab; leaped in and directed the driver to break all speed laws to the municipal airport. The taxicab driver started to give Gillian a scornful look, then recognized him; ticked his forefinger to the vizor of his cap and said: "You bet, Mr. Hazeltine!"

At the field office of the airport, Gillian spoke brusquely to a blue-eyed young man.

"I want to charter a two-passenger plane for the night—that is, a plane which will carry two people beside the pilot. I want a pilot who can make a safe landing after dark in a field no larger than a backyard."

"There's a pilot here from the Long Island Curtiss Field," stated the field manager. "He's Randy Enslow. Randy used to barnstorm with Lindbergh in the old days before Slim went into the air mail. Randy could fly a wheelbarrow."

Twenty minutes later, Gillian followed a tall, lean young

man with a snub nose and clear gray eyes into the cabin of a yellow monoplane. Its engine roared. Gillian settled himself in an uncomfortable seat and watched the instrument board and the back of Randy Enslow's neck.

Enslow was taxiing the monoplane to the end of the field, ducking his head from side to side. Gillian placed his hands upon his stomach and tried to compose his interior. He had flown only once or twice, and he did not like the sensation.

The motor suddenly roared more loudly than it had before. The ground began skimming along below Gillian's fascinated eyes. Then something else skimmed below Gillian's fascinated eyes—several hangars. He looked down the right wing and his stomach receded within him still more. The wing was pointing straight at the hangars.

The yellow monoplane straightened out of the sharp turn and headed north. Gillian settled back and appreciated the young man in the seat in front of him. A great race of men, these flyers. Took it as casually as he took driving his car.

Darkness fell. Lights sprang into being on the earth below. A moon came up in the east and Gillian fell to thinking of Vee-Anne. He dozed. He awoke, startled. A man was squeezing his foot. The roar of the engine was absent. In its place was a singing of wind.

Enslow's voice: "That the place?"

Gillian looked down. The moon had risen, lost its redness and become a source of silver light. It was shining on a long oval of water. On the far bank was the dark huddle of a house.

Gillian shouted: "Yes! That house. There's a ten-acre wheat field behind it."

The motor roared again. The yellow monoplane climbed. Enslow opened a window and tossed something overboard. It was a parachute flare. The light descended slowly, radiating the wheat field with a pure white glare. The plane began doing things. Its nose went down. Its right wing went up. It went corkscrewing to earth. Lights flashed on under its fuselage—landing lights. A hundred feet above the field, the pilot put the ship into a fast sideslip. Then it straightened. It landed in the field with a bump so slight that Gillian was hardly aware of it.

"Wait," he said to Enslow. "Have you enough fuel to fly back to Greenboro?"

"Plenty," said the pilot.

Gillian started across the field toward the house. Half way there, a figure in pale-gray knickerbockers met him. Henshaw said:

"Well, I'll be damned!"

"You're flying back with me," said Gillian grimly. "We're starting at once."

"Gillian, I'm not going to testify for that skunk. That's final."

"You've had a brainstorm," said Gillian. "Snap out of it."

"I've been thinking," the publisher disagreed. "If you let Robard go, sooner or later he'll be back, bleeding me again. Let him die in the chair!"

"That," Gillian snapped, "would be deliberate murder."

"Death is what he deserves."

"Half your life," Gillian said coldly, "you've regretted murdering one man. You may be willing to take another murder upon your conscience—but I won't. I told you, I will not be a party to any murder."

The publisher's shoulders seemed to sag. He said, in a tired voice:

"I've tried all my life to be a square shooter. Since that night in San Francisco, I've never laid my finger on a man in anger. And for fifteen years that reptile has been stabbing me in the back. But I'll go with you, Gillian. I'll testify for him."

8

SURPRISE WITNESS

DON ROBARD, WITH furtive, suspicious eyes, stared at
Gillian as Gillian made his opening address to the jury.

Mr. Yistle sat back in his chair and watched Gillian
with half-lidded eyes of complacency and amusement.
He turned presently and whispered to his assistant, Mr.
Bullock:

"Now, for some high-powered spellbinding. But it won't
get him anywhere. Gillian is licked and he's going to stay
licked. We've got him sewed up in a bag, Mr. Bullock!"

"Yes, *sir!*" affirmed Mr. Bullock, who was an incurable
yes-man.

Said Gillian: "… And I will endeavor to prove to you,
ladies and gentlemen of the jury, that the testimony of
apparently reliable eye and ear witnesses is not always to
be depended upon. I will endeavor to establish beyond
the shadow of a doubt that Don Robard was not within
miles of the old salt dock on the night when Herman
Ochas came to his death. My first witness will be Charles
Murchison."

There was an audible stir in the court room as Charles
Murchison, the proprietor of the hot-dog stand on River

Street, made his way to the stand. He seated himself and looked at Gillian uneasily.

Gillian said sharply: "Mr. Murchison, yesterday when you took the stand, you said that at about ten thirty on the night of September 16 Herman Ochas and a man entered your restaurant and ordered coffee and doughnuts."

"Yes, sir."

"You said further that your eyesight is excellent."

"Yes, sir; I said that."

"Mr. Murchison," Gillian said gently, "you don't want to be arrested and sent to jail for perjury, do you?"

Mr. Yistle leaped up and cried: "Objection!"

"Overruled. The defense will proceed. The witness will answer that question."

The man with the toothbrush mustache answered: "No, sir; I don't want to be arrested for perjury."

"Then, Mr, Murchison, wouldn't you like to retract the statement you made yesterday that your eyes are excellent?"

Mr. Murchison looked at Gillian unhappily and said nothing.

"Wouldn't you," Gillian urged him, "like to tell this jury the truth about your eyes. That you are so shortsighted you cannot even read a newspaper without your glasses? Isn't that the truth?"

"Yes, sir; that's the truth."

"Then, why did you testify yesterday that your eyes are so good?"

"Because I'm ashamed of them bein' so bad."

Gillian looked at him sternly. "Mr. Murchison, on the night when Herman Ochas and *some man* came into your restaurant, isn't it true that you were *not* wearing your glasses?"

"Yes, sir; it's true. I left my glasses at home that night."

"Then you will admit that you cannot be absolutely certain that the man who entered your restaurant with Herman Ochas was this man sitting here?"

"I guess I'll have to admit that, Mr. Hazeltine."

"Wouldn't you like to say, Mr. Murchison, that you are not at all certain that the man who entered the restaurant with Herman Ochas was Don Robard?"

"I guess I'd better be on the safe side and say that I'm not at all certain," agreed the willing witness.

"That will be all," said Gillian.

MR. YISTLE TOOK the witness. He took him in a spirit of indignation and rage. He took Mr Murchison back and forth across his testimony of yesterday, but the hot-dog stand proprietor became more and more conservative. He became less and less certain that the man with Herman Ochas had been black-haired. He might have been blond. He was sorry. He had only wanted to help the cause of justice.

Finally, in a fine fury, Mr. Yistle dismissed him. He sat down and glared at Gillian, and Gillian gave him a round-eyed, innocent stare in return.

The Court: "Call your next witness."

Gillian's next witness was Maggie O'Toole. The old Irishwoman took the stand very pertly this morning.

"Mrs. O'Toole," Gillian began, "when you took the stand yesterday, isn't it true that you were a little excited, that you may have made certain statements that you would like to retract to-day?"

"I won't say that I would," retorted the Irish lady. "No. I won't say anything of the kind."

"I would like to refresh your memory, Mrs. O'Toole. Isn't it true that on the night of last June 10, and on the night of last July 12 and on the night of last August 4, you were taken to night court to answer to a drunkenness charge?"

"Well," snapped the Irish lady, "what of it?"

"Isn't it true that on the night of September 16, shortly before you left your work in the Atchison Building, one of the tenants, a stockbroker, working late, gave you a pint flask of rye whisky?"

"He is a perfect gentleman," stated Maggie O'Toole belligerently.

"Isn't it true that, in his presence, you drank practically the entire contents of that pint flask of rye whisky?"

Maggie O'Toole looked at Gillian defiantly. But she said nothing.

"Isn't it true," he persisted, coming closer to her, "that when you walked home from work that night you were seeing double?"

"I never see double!" Maggie shouted. "I may see things blurred, but I never see things double!"

"Very well—blurred. On the night of September 16, as you staggered home from work, you passed two men on River Street. One of them you recognized as Herman Ochas. The other you say you now identify as the accused."

"That's what I said," agreed Maggie, but there was much less assurance in her voice.

"But how can you be so certain that this was the man with Herman Ochas when everything before your eyes was so blurred?"

"I suppose I can't be so certain," Maggie admitted.

"That will be all," said Gillian.

Mr. Yistle's indignation was mounting. His face was now pink. It soon became crimson as he cross-examined Maggie O'Toole. No; she hadn't told any lies yesterday. No; she didn't realize that she may have perjured herself. No, no, no; she wouldn't swear to-day that the men she saw on River Street that night were Herman Ochas and Don Robard. She wasn't even certain that one of the men was Herman Ochas. Things were pretty blurred that night.

The district attorney ended his cross-examination in a sputtering outburst. He wanted this witness held for perjury.

"Decision reserved," ruled Judge Helman, and to Gillian: "Call your next witness."

GILLIAN'S NEXT WITNESS was the gorilla man. Nick Whaley came lumbering to the stand. His small, close-set eyes seemed to be slightly crossed as they fixed themselves on Gillian.

"Mr. Whaley," Gillian sharply began, "yesterday when you testified, you stated that on your eleven o'clock rounds on the night of September 16, you saw Herman Ochas and another man standing near an old shack or shed or shanty on the old salt dock, engaged in conversation. You said that you flashed your light on them, and that you recognized Herman Ochas and that, since then, you have identified the other man as Don Robard. I want you to answer a question honestly: Since that night, have you ever seen that other man until yesterday, when you pointed him out in court?"

"No, sir; I never saw him in between."

"And you recognized him yesterday as the man who was with Herman Ochas on the night in question."

"I thought I did, sir."

"What do you mean," Mr. Yistle snapped, "you thought you did?"

"Your honor," said Gillian, "the esteemed district attorney for the people may take this witness for cross-examination when I have finished with him."

Mr. Yistle's face had turned alarmingly from pink to cerise. He seemed to have difficulty with his breathing. But he subsided.

Gillian: "But I will repeat Mr. Yistle's question. It is a fair one. What do you mean—you *thought* you did?"

The witness fumbled with his hairy hands.

"I mean that when I got to thinkin' it over, I wasn't so sure. The more I thought about it, the surer I was that the feller I seen with Herman that night was a blond feller, with blue eyes, and this feller here has black hair and brown eyes."

Mr. Yistle expressed his feelings with a snort that was heard distinctly in the farthest corner of the court room.

"And when you returned to the old salt dock on your twelve o'clock rounds," Gillian pursued, "what did you see of Herman Ochas's companion then?"

"I didn't see him. No. I didn't see him at all."

"But, damn it," exclaimed the furious district attorney, "you said yesterday—"

"Silence!" ordered Judge Helman. "You may take this witness for cross-examination at the proper time, Mr. Yistle."

Mr. Yistle subsided, fuming. He went into a conference of heated whisperings with Mr. Bullock, but nothing seemed to come of it.

"Then," Gillian was saying to the witness, "you are not certain that the man who fired the shot that killed Herman Ochas was Don Robard. Might there not have been two or three men with him in the darkness at the end of the dock?"

"Yes, sir; there might have been."

"You fell down, didn't you, and were so dazed that you weren't very clear in your mind just what was going on?"

"That's the truth!" exclaimed the gorilla man.

"And you are fairly certain that the man with whom Herman Ochas was talking, on your eleven o'clock rounds, was blond and blue eyed?"

"Yes, sir; I'm pretty positive about it now."

"That will be all," said Gillian.

And once again Mr. Yistle leaped up, determined to save his burning bridges, and to plug the holes in his dyke. But the witness had become taciturn. No, he wasn't certain of anything. No, he wasn't certain he had seen the murderer running up Polk Street. Yes, he was positive there had been a gang of men at the foot of the dock when the shot was fired. Mr. Yistle gave it up in despair. He muttered references under his breath to perjurers, and Gillian in a clear, ringing voice announced:

"My next witness is Mr. Victor Henshaw."

EVEN MR. YISTLE, steeped in fury and gloom, looked up at that. Heads turned. Necks craned.

There was a spattering of applause. Victor Henshaw was easily the most popular public figure in Greenboro. His newspaper was clean and just and courageous; it stood for decency and right and fairness.

The man who had been responsible for the moderniz-
ing of the Greenboro public schools, for numerous public
libraries, for at least two new hospitals and for the splendid
city park system, came striding down the aisle.

Victor Henshaw gazed at the judge. Judge Helman
gazed at him. Not a spark of recognition was visible in
either man's eyes. You would never have suspected that
they and certain other prominent citizens of Greenboro
met every Thursday night and played dollar limit stud—
and had been doing so for years.

Mr. Henshaw took the stand and turned his fierce amber
eyes first on Mr. Yistle, then on Gillian. Don Robard he
ignored. And the blackmailer glared at him with beseech-
ing eyes.

The publisher of the Greenboro *Times* was sworn.
Gillian fired questions at him:

"Where were you, Mr. Henshaw, at ten thirty o'clock on
the night of September 16?"

"I was sitting on my veranda, smoking a cigar."

"Did you have a caller?"

"I did."

"Who was this caller?"

"Don Robard."

"You are certain your caller was Don Robard and that
the time he arrived was ten thirty?"

"Of course I am certain," was the harsh answer.

"Will you kindly tell the jury what had transpired that
evening?"

Victor Henshaw faced the jury.

"Nothing in particular transpired. I had seen Don
Robard on the golf course at the country club that after-

noon. He had said he wished to drop in late that evening and talk over certain investments. At ten thirty he arrived. We talked until some time after twelve thirty. I should say, between half past twelve and a quarter to one, Don Robard left my house."

"That will be all," said Gillian. The defense rests."

9

SCOTCHING A SNAKE

THE DISTRICT ATTORNEY sat staring at Victor Henshaw. His lips were moving. Sounds came from them. But these sounds were not words. They were emotions. It could almost be said that steam was issuing from Mr. Yistle's open mouth. But he presently took himself in hand and walked to the bench.

"Your honor," he exclaimed, "I smell a rat here. I smell a whole family of rats. I have been made the butt of a cruel, practical joke. I wish to have Charles Murchison, Maggie O'Toole and Nick Whaley arraigned and charged with perjury. I will bring the charges."

"You do not," his honor asked with what seemed to be surprise, "wish to cross-examine Mr. Henshaw?"

"Naturally, I do not!" sputtered the indignant district attorney.

"Mr. Hazeltine," said Judge Helman sharply, "will you step up here, please?"

Gillian complied. Judge Helman fixed him with what could be best described as an oystery look.

"Gillian," he said in a low voice, "why didn't you want that reptile electrocuted? You know damned well he deserved it!"

"I have other plans for him," Gillian answered.

Judge Helman again became a stem member of the judiciary.

"Mr. Yistle, I am afraid I must deny your petition. I can see no reason bringing perjury charges against these witnesses. They are all excused."

The judge now made one of the briefest charges to a jury on record in the archives of any court house. He said:

"Ladies and gentlemen of the jury, it will not be necessary for you to retire to deliberate upon the testimony you have heard."

"No, your honor," said the foreman.

The clerk of the court went through the ancient formula of the Court of Oyer and Terminer. Standing up with his book, he polled the twelve standing men and women, and the court crier gave back their numbers in echo to their names.

"Gentlemen and ladies of the jury," chanted the clerk, "have you arrived at a verdict for Don Robard?"

"We have."

"How say you?"

The slow, rumbling voice of the foreman: "Not guilty."

Mr. Yistle in a loud voice moved that the verdict be set aside. His petition was curtly denied by the judge.

Don Robard stood up dazedly. But there was no smile on his lips. He was trembling. He was watching Gillian with eyes which were those of a whipped animal.

"I'll say good-by," he said.

"Not yet," said Gillian. "We're going for a little ride."

Victor Henshaw came walking over. He ignored Robard.

"I suppose, Gillian, that you will attend to this reptile."

"He'll never annoy you again," Gillian promised. "You'll never see his face again. Because, if you do, there will be witnesses who won't change their minds so easily. Robard understands that—don't you, Robard?"

"Yes—I understand," said Robard, and in his eyes was still reflected the terror of the fate he had so narrowly escaped.

"You're through with me, Gillian?" asked Henshaw.

Gillian nodded. And grinned. "Vic, was it a better way out than a tailspin?"

"Far better," the publisher agreed.

"NOW," SAID GILLIAN to Robard, "you're coming with me."

Don Robard looked frightened. He started to protest, then fell into step beside Gillian. Gillian took him around to the rear of the courthouse where his coupé was parked. He told Robard to climb in.

"Where are you taking me?"

"For a little ride."

"You mean—you're going to kill me?"

"Sit down and shut up," said Gillian grimly.

Gillian shut the door and tooled the long, gray coupé through the afternoon traffic and out toward the Riverdale Development. He turned into his own driveway presently and stopped at the side porch steps.

Gillian alighted and said: "Come with me, Robard."

Don Robard obeyed. He followed Gillian into the house. In the living room Gillian found Toro polishing furniture.

"Where is Mrs. Hazeltine?"

"In the garden, sir."

"Come," Gillian growled.

Robard came. He followed Gillian, as a dog follows its master, through the house and out upon the terrace; across the terrace and into a sunken garden which blazed with the autumnal colors of chrysanthemum, snapdragon, and the last dahlias.

Vee-Anne, in a white dress over which she wore a blue apron, was cutting chrysanthemums. She turned about swiftly as the two men came toward her. Her eyes, as she saw Don Robard, narrowed and hardened until they were two narrow strips of emerald.

"So you got him off!" she exclaimed.

Gillian nodded soberly. The speech he had prepared he knew he could not deliver. He had planned to say: "Vee-Anne, here he is—here's your lover. You are free to do what you wish. But I think the two of you had better not stay in Greenboro."

He did not say that; and Gillian would be glad to the day of his death that he did not say that—or anything like it. For Vee-Anne's next words all but rendered Gillian breathless.

"What a pity!" she cried. "If ever a man deserved to be sent to the electric chair, it's this man."

Vee-Anne laid the flowers and the shears on the grass at her feet She straightened up and placed her hands upon her hips.

"What," she asked, "are you going to do with him?"

"He is leaving Greenboro," said Gillian weakly, still looking dazed. "He is leaving Greenboro at once. And never coming back."

Vee-Anne gazed up into her husband's face searchingly. A tiny groove between her eyes; a slight arching of her brows. She brushed a strand of coppery hair from her white forehead.

"Gillian, what were you up to?"

Gillian pretended not to understand. His eyes became round and innocent. The line between Vee-Anne's eyes deepened.

"You didn't fool me for a moment—not after that trial had started," she went on. "That whole trial was a frame-up. The three witnesses who testified for the State would lay down their lives for you—or, let's say, lie themselves black in the face for you. Charlie Murchison, who runs that hot-dog stand—you got his son out of the reform school, didn't you?"

"Well, as a matter of fact—" Gillian lamely began.

"And Maggie O'Toole," proceeded the red-haired girl; "you've got job after job for her, in spite of the way the poor old thing drinks. Haven't you? And didn't you intervene one time when she was sentenced to six months in the workhouse?"

"Now, listen, Vee-Anne—" Gillian began again.

"And didn't you save Nick Whaley's brother Jim from a possible ten-year sentence about five years ago when he was mixed up with those silk thieves?"

"Jim Whaley never stole that silk!" Gillian declared.

"Darling, don't try to bluff me. I'm merely saying that those three people would lay down their lives for you. So you primed them beautifully and sent them to poor Bert Yistle as witnesses against Don Robard. But why, Gillian?"

"He was trying to blackmail a friend of mine. In fact, he was blackmailing him."

"IS THAT WHY you've been acting so strangely the past few weeks since Robard was arrested?"

Gillian did not answer. Vee-Anne seemed puzzled.

"Or was it because you had heard rumors about Don Robard and me?"

"Well," Gillian admitted, "I had heard rumors."

"Ugly rumors?"

"Well, yes, they weren't nice rumors. Rumors seldom are."

"And all this time you've been treating me just the same as ever!"

"You see—" Gillian tried to explain. But Vee-Anne stopped him again.

"I was hoping it wouldn't be necessary to explain anything. I knew that, regardless of anything you heard about me and Don Robard or any other man, you would have faith in me. You would know that the only man in the world I could possibly love would be you."

Gillian was beginning to feel a little giddy. After all these weeks of torture—

Vee-Anne was saying: "You heard that I had been to his apartment. You heard many such things. Well, I may as well make a clean breast of everything. After the lesson you've taught him, I don't believe Don Robard will practice blackmail soon again in this community. Gillian, I was on his list, too. I didn't tell you—I didn't want to worry you, but Tom has been writing bad checks again."

Tom was Vee-Anne's half-brother, a scamp.

"I covered the checks, but there was trouble, anyway. And Don Robard got wind of it. And he threatened to expose Tom, knowing that any such publicity would be injurious to you—and would be painful for me. I think Tom has learned his lesson. He had a dreadful scare. Well, darling, that's all. No; it isn't quite all. I'm not the only person in this city that Robard had been blackmailing."

"I assure you that this charming community need worry about me no longer," Don Robard said.

Gillian gazed at him with round, innocent eyes.

"Robard," he said slowly, "you don't know what you're talking about. This community isn't worrying about you. You had better get busy and worry about the community. If you once again put foot in this community, you will undergo an experience which will make what you've been through these past two days seem as charming and delightful as Alice's trip through Wonderland. You will never realize how close you came to the electric chair.

"I am giving you until midnight to-night to get out of town. If you are not out of town by midnight to-night, you will regret it. If you ever return, or if you ever attempt to correspond with any one in this town—I will stamp on you again. And there won't be a wiggle or a squirm left in you."

Don Robard looked at Gillian, and he looked at Vee-Anne. He started to smile, but his lips shook so that he could not smile. He wanted to say something nasty, something crushing; but his courage failed him.

"One more point," Gillian went on. "Wherever you go, if a rumor comes to me that you have spoken to any one about a certain incident in the past of a certain man—I'll reach halfway around the world and bring you back here to suffer for it. Do we understand each other?"

"Yes," gasped Robard.

"Clear out of here!"

Robard departed.

Vee-Anne was looking up at Gillian curiously. She said:

"In the thick of all those ugly rumors, did you for a moment doubt me, Gillian?"

Gillian took her in his arms and kissed her. His experience had taught him that the best answer to such a question is a long, ardent kiss.

THE LOST PUNCH

*When Fate stacked things against fighting
Tim Bunce, Gillian Hazeltine took a hand
in the game—and made ring history*

1

BATTLING BUNCE

GILLIAN HAZELTINE CLOSED the door, walked over to his desk and selected from a silver humidor a slender blond cigar. Every Christmas the famous criminal lawyer received a thousand of these cigars from a wealthy client whom he had cleverly saved from the electric chair. The client, it chanced, had been innocent.

When the cigar was glowing, he seated himself and looked amiably at the worried little bright-eyed, pink-cheeked Irishman who was perched like a bird on the edge of the chair beside the desk.

"Well, Paddy?"

Paddy Tobin, trainer and manager of prize fighters, nervously cleared his throat. He looked as if he hadn't had much sleep lately. His face was drawn and there were pouches under his eyes.

"Mr. Hazeltine, one of my boys is in a jam. It's a difficult case, and it's a strange case. It isn't a case for the law courts, but early this morning, after lying awake all night worrying, I decided that you are the one man who can tell us what to do. The lad's name is Tim Bunce. He fights under the name of Battling Bunce."

"The name," said Gillian, "is familiar. What's his class and what's his trouble?"

"Bunce has only been in the fight racket about a year," the trainer answered. "He has been fighting in preliminaries. If I were to tell you how good he was before this trouble happened, you would not believe me."

"I would believe anything *you* told me about any fighter," said Gillian.

"Tim Bunce came to me," Paddy went on, "under somewhat unusual circumstances. A girl whose father I know well—Mike Kelly, a cop on the gas-house beat—came to me about a year ago and said that she was going to bring around a young fellow who was a natural-born killer. She said he was her boy-friend and that she had discovered, after keeping company with him for a couple of years, that he was a two-fisted mauler. It seems they had gone up the river on the Idlewild on one of the Sunday night excursions, and during the trip back a crowd of young rowdies, four or five of them, had been razzing her and Bunce. You know where the Idlewild docks, Mr. Hazeltine—down by the old iron ore dock?"

Gillian nodded.

"WELL," PADDY WENT on, "when the passengers got off, this gang of roughnecks decided they were going to take Kitty away from Tim. And they tried to. They rushed Tim. Kitty said that the way her boy went into action was like what might happen if you tossed four or five fat rabbits into the cage of a starving wild cat.

"When the smoke cleared, three of those young gorillas were stretched out—knocked out cold: one of the others

Tim said later that he didn't hear the warning

was having a terrible hemorrhage from the nose, and the ringleader wore a pair of purple eyes for the next two weeks.

"Up to that time, Tim Bunce had been nothing in the world but a shipping clerk down at Harnegan's. He had done some boxing, in a friendly way, but apparently nobody had ever discovered that he had a pair of mule hoofs in each hand.

"Knowing how girls are apt to boast about their boy-friends, I was pretty skeptical. But I told Kitty to bring the boy around. Next evening she brought him up to my gym. He was as clean-cut and well-built a light heavy-weight as you ever clapped an eye on; good shoulders, a good head and a good eye. If there was anything wrong with him, it was his modesty. When it came to his own talents, he was a natural born pooh-pooher. Well, you've seen Lefty Schmidt in the ring, haven't you?"

Gillian, with his hands clasped comfortably behind his head, his blond cigar jutting out from his mouth at a rakish angle, nodded. "He's a dirty fighter, but a good one."

"Yes, sir; dirty but good. He was training for his bout with Jim Walker at that time. I asked him if he would put on the gloves with Bunce and see what he had. So the boys put them on. Mr. Hazeltine, you would not have believed it unless you had seen it. Bunce had hardly any style. His footwork was terrible. His stance would have made you laugh out loud; but he walked right into Lefty and he one-twoed him all over that ring! He hit him with everything but the ring posts and buckets. I yelled at Lefty: 'You needn't pull 'em any more. Let's see how he can take 'em now.' And Lefty puffed at me: 'What—do you think I'm doin' this on purpose? Call this mad dog off!'

"And that, Mr. Hazeltine, was how I came to know I had found a natural. In all my ring experience, it was the first time it ever happened. Without an invitation, I had had a boy walk into my gymnasium who had the makings of another Dempsey. That boy had everything! Everything but finish. He had a punch in his two hands like a steam roller swinging on the end of a steel cable. And he loved to fight. And he had the other things: clean-looking, but not too good-looking, and modesty. Another thing: he was built long and lean and rangy, and he weighed a hundred and seventy-two. With careful training, he would work up nicely as a heavyweight."

"WHY," GILLIAN DRYLY intruded, "have you been keeping this bright light of yours under a bushel?"

"In the first place," Paddy promptly answered, "I did not want to force him. He was worth a slow building up. I wanted to take my time to teach him form and style. Before he went into the big limelight, I wanted him to be the classiest boy that ever stepped through the ropes. Also, he was too modest. So I started him off easy. When he was already good enough to draw an even break with Jake Mullin and Frankie Walsh, I was keeping him in preliminaries. He has never been in a star bout. I never let him cut loose. I never let him take his man before the third round. I kept him down. At the beginning of the third round, or sometimes even the fourth, I would say: 'All right, Timmy; wipe him up.' And Timmy would go in there and one-two him to death before you knew what was happening.

"I tell you, Mr. Hazeltine, the boy is a born killer! And absolutely obedient and manageable. When he knew how good he was, he did not get a swelled head. He had just one weakness, and that was Kitty Kelly; only it wasn't exactly a weakness. He was crazy about Kitty. And Kitty could handle that big blond cave man as if he was a baby. It was a case of true love on both sides. Kitty knew how good the boy was, but she agreed absolutely with me. He mustn't be forced. Let him take things easy until he was so classy that he would knock them off their feet.

"His girl and I weren't the only ones in on the secret. One day, when the boy was working out up at the gym with Tiger Wales, the colored heavyweight, Jake Mullin dropped in. Jake had just won the light heavyweight championship and he was feeling pretty cocky about it. Jake is a slob anyway. And a snake.

"Jake stood there by the ring, watching the workout, and pretty soon he turned to me and said: 'Paddy, I'd like to put them on with that blond wonder of yours.' Well, Mr. Hazeltine, you know how boys are. When I told Tim that the champion wanted to put on the gloves with him, he was tickled and flattered silly. He thought it was a great honor. And I said: 'Never mind the honor stuff. Watch out for that right of his. He used to work in the stockyards, and they say when he got tired of killing beef with a sledge hammer, he used that right.'

"Well, they put them on, Mr. Hazeltine. And Jake Mullin, without a word of warning, let go with that right. He let it go right where he always tries to let it go—into the pit of the stomach.

"Tim saw it coming, and he blocked it with his left, but the force of it sent the boy halfway across the ring. That honored grin came right off, and he went after the big-hearted champion in a way that reminded you of a mother leopard coming out of her cave to defend her young. One-two! One-two! He chased Mr. Champion all over that ring. Finally, he got him into a corner and began lamming away, first to the belly, then to the jaw. But he wasn't quite fast enough for that right. It came up into his face like an exploding flywheel.

"It was the best Jake Mullin had. I doubt if he ever, in any of his knockouts, put over that right so well timed or so hard. It connected with the boy's chin. Down he went! But did he stay down? Nobody was counting, but when you have been in the fight racket as long as I have, you develop a stop-watch instinct in the back of your brain. Mine was ticking them off: one—two—three—four—five—six—

"At six, the boy shook his head. At eight, he rolled over onto his hands and knees. At nine, his gloves were off the floor. But Jake Mullin was out of the ring by then, and saying to me: 'Not half bad, Paddy. That boy is pretty good.' Pretty good! I will tell the world that he is pretty good!"

PADDY NODDED EMPHATICALLY, and then slowly went

on: "It was right after that, Mr. Hazeltine, that the trouble began. Jake Mullin met Kitty. And Kitty didn't lose much time getting his goat. You know how the women flock around a champion. Well, Kitty wasn't the flocking kind. She was in love with Tim, and she didn't have any time for Mullin. She told him to roll his hoop. Pretty soon, he wanted her as he'd never wanted anything before in his crooked life. After awhile, he wanted to marry her.

"Kitty kept shoving him off, and saying she didn't even like him, let alone love him. But when he pulled the marriage stuff, it made things different. Not with her. But her mother, her old man, and her two good-for-nothing brothers began taking sides with Mullin. They began riding her. Why was she waiting around for a palooka like Tim Bunce, when she could grab off a gilt-edged guy like Mullin? A real champion!

"They hammered and dinged and harped away at the poor kid until she began to look like a little wreck. Her old man was the worst. You know how prize fighters stand in with the cops, anyway. And old man Kelly was so flattered to have the light heavyweight champ paying attentions to his daughter that he couldn't see straight. Here, he says, is a great chance for her to marry well. A million girls he could name, he says, would snap at the chance."

"Did you," Gillian interrupted, "argue with Kelly?"

"I did! I argued myself black and blue and in circles. I told him that, given a year's more time, Tim would be at the top of the light heavy division. I told him he would keep puttin' on weight and would, in three years at the outside, be a sensation in heavyweight circles. And he said I was just handing out the usual applesauce of every fight manager.

"Kitty was a stenog then, down in Minturn's brokerage office. She had to be on the job at 9 A.M. Mr. Hazeltine, her old man and those worthless brothers of hers used to keep her out of bed till four and five and six in the morning, wrangling at her about Mullin.

"They finally barred Tim Bunce out of the house, and he and Kitty had to meet on the sly, the poor kids. I'm no softhearted sentimentalist, Mr. Hazeltine, but I sure did feel sorry for those kids. They were so crazy about each other, it was pathetic. They used to meet up at the gym, and they just used to sit there in my office, holding hands and not saying anything. Sometimes it made me so mad I could have used a sawed-off shotgun on Mullin and that whole blamed Kelly family. I used to ask them why didn't they run off and get married and to the deuce with the family. But Kitty said no, they had made a sacred agreement not to get married until after Tim had won his first star bout.

"If I had had any sense, I would have built up a star bout for Tim right then—any star bout, and I would have picked a palooka that Tim could take in one soft punch with an eight-ounce glove. But I didn't realize then that Kitty was cracking so fast under the strain.

"One morning, about seven o'clock, I got a telephone call at my boarding house from Kitty. She was having hysterics, laughing and crying. She says she couldn't stand it any longer; she hadn't had three hours' sleep in the past week, and she guessed she was just a weak woman and a coward and a quitter; but things looked so hopeless, she had given in. She said to tell Tim she loved him and she would never love anybody else, but she was going to buy a little peace by marrying Mullin. 'Break the news to Tim,' she says.

'Tell him it's too late to do anything.' Then she began to cry, and I heard some man yelling at her, and she hung up." Gillian nodded.

"THAT WAS FIVE weeks ago, Mr. Hazeltine," Paddy resumed. "And if what she got was peace, give me war, with liquid fire, mustard gas and all the trimmings! The minute Mullin married her, things were different. His true nature began coming out. It makes me squirm when I think about it. I don't see how any man can treat a girl the way Mullin has treated Kitty. I wish you could see her! Before all this started, she was always pink-cheeked and jolly and full of fun. She was always joking and kidding everybody, and she was always poking fun at Tim the way girls do when they're crazy about a boy. Now, all the life has gone out of her. All the color out of her cheeks. All the sparkle. Big circles under her eyes. She's so white and thin that it just makes you sick to look at her.

"She called Tim up quite a few times, to tell him what a little fool she had been and that she still loved him. The boy just went to pieces. Well, how would you like to have the girl you are crazy about call you up at three in the morning, crying her eyes-out, because her husband had just beat her up till she fainted? What could you do? It's none of your business, is it? He's her husband, isn't he? You keep your nose out of married people's scraps, don't you? Would you have him arrested and drag her name through the tabloids?"

"You might come to a lawyer, as you have done," said Gillian dryly.

"I didn't come to you about that," said Paddy. "Wait till you hear the rest of it. If you don't want to jump in and do all you can for Tim Bunce, then you are a different man than I think you are. Yesterday morning, Mullin tried to kill Tim. Tim is outside in your waiting room. We will send for him in a minute. But I want to tell you the rest of it before you look him over. You may tell him there is nothing to do but to kill Mullin. I mean, it is as serious as that. And if you say, kill Mullin, we will kill Mullin!"

2

IN THE TRAINING CAMP

GILLIAN'S BLOND CIGAR had gone out. He relighted it. Whispers of this amazing story that Paddy Tobin was telling him had reached him through underground sources. But he wanted the complete story from Paddy before he made any comment.

"I know now," Paddy went on, "that Mullin is one of these men who get a big kick out of hurting people and seeing them suffer. I have checked up on him. He was always a bully. Even when he was a kid, he was always hurting kids smaller than himself.

"You know, of course, that Mullin is slated to meet Frankie Walsh on the Fourth of July. When Mullin went into training a little over a week ago, he came to see me. He said he wanted to borrow Tim as a sparring partner. Frankie Walsh is a left-hander, and Tim's left is as good as his right; also, Tim is about Walsh's size, and his fighting style is about the same. He is a mixer, like Jack Dempsey. So is Walsh. All in all, said Mullin, Tim would make a fine sparring partner for him.

"Of course I said absolutely nothing doing. Tim was in bad enough shape as it was, without being dragged into that mess. I knew that Kitty was out there at Mullin's camp, living with him in his little cottage there. I knew Tim and she would somehow see each other—and hell would be popping. I didn't want Tim to get hurt, anyway.

"While we were arguing it, Tim came in; and Mullin put it up to him. He told Tim just what he had told me, and added: 'Kiddo, here is a dandy chance for you to work out a defense against that right of mine. One of these days, if you keep getting good, you and I may meet under the bright lights. When that night comes, you want to be able to keep away from me and keep me away from you. How about it?'

"The poor kid didn't hesitate. I knew he wasn't thinking of Mullin's arguments at all. He was thinking of being up there near Kitty—as if it would do him a bit of good! I talked myself black in the face, but it didn't do any good. When Mullin went, Tim went with him. And I tagged along. I didn't want that boy crucified by that big ape if I could help it.

"What happened was just what I figured would happen. I will say for Mullin that he is smart. He is too damned smart. It is the kind of smartness that puts men back of bars, where they belong. I am sure he got a cruel kind of pleasure in seeing Kitty and Tim face to face across the dining room table. He would make ugly little cracks to them about married life, and how sweet and loving Kitty was when she had her arms around his neck at night.

"I will say for Tim that he acted every minute like a gentleman. I used to see the red shoot up into his face and ears when Mullin's rough stuff got too rough. Tim is a better gentleman than these college-made gentlemen: he is a born gentleman. He kept his mouth shut and did his work.

"And that was where this strange thing happened. At the beginning of that week, it was a toss-up which man was the better fighter. Tim used to one-two Mullin around that ring in a way that was a pleasure for tired eyes. And he kept blocking that right, blocking it until Mullin almost went nuts. Of course, they wore face guards. All the time they were in there, Mullin was razzing the kid; talking to him in whispers. And the kid would not tell me what it was that Mullin was saying. But by the middle of the week, the kid cracked. It didn't happen suddenly. It was slow. His punches began losing their power; his timing began to be bad, and his defense fell off. To me, watching, it was like watching a great solid rock crumbling to pieces for no reason at all."

HAZELTINE BROKE IN: "In this time, did Bunce have any talks with Kitty?"

"No, sir; I was coming to that. He didn't try to talk to her, and she didn't try to talk to him. They treated each other politely. He called her Mrs. Mullin, and she called him Tim. They weren't cold or distant or over-polite; they were just behaving the way any lady and gentleman would behave. You would have thought that there had never been anything more between them than boy and girl friendship. But I bunked in the room with Tim, and I knew different. I would hear him tossing about in his bed, and sometimes groaning or talking in his sleep. And it just made me sick. Mullin might just as well have carved his heart out with a knife.

"Tim did not try to see Kitty on the sly. But one morning, yesterday morning it was, she sent him a note by the dishwasher. She said she must see him, so he told the dishwasher to tell her he would manage it in a few minutes.

"Every morning, when Mullin went out for road work, he made Tim go along, to keep an eye on him. Yesterday, when they started out, Tim went to the first turn in the road, lagging behind. He kept lagging behind, and at the first turn, he dropped out, cut across a field and went to Mullin's cottage.

"Kitty was sitting there on the steps, huddled up against a roof post, her eyes all red from crying. Tim sat down beside her and she says: 'Tim, isn't there anything we can do? I just can't stand it. Look at this!'

"Well, Mr. Hazeltine, Tim looked. She was wearing a dress with long sleeves. She pulled up the sleeves and her arms were one solid mass of black-and-blue marks and bruises. She said she was like that almost all over her body. Mullin had got sore at her last night, and started accusin' her of seein' Tim on the sly, and for the first time she sassed him back. She said he had spoiled her life and Tim's life, and she hated him like the snake he was. And Mullin lit into her. He hit her and he kicked her. Well, I won't go into the details, Mr. Hazeltine.

"The kid finally said to her: 'We have played this thing straight, Kitty. But we are through playing it straight. You are going to pack up. We are going away, and to hell with everything and everybody. We will go West or somewhere.'

"He stopped right there. And the reason he stopped was that Mullin was standin' there right in front of them, with a mean grin on his ugly pan. He had his hands on his hips, and in that dirty white sweatshirt, he looked nine feet tall and six feet wide.

"His jaw was shoved out, and he was grinning at Tim. Tim jumped right up, ready for a knock-down-and-drag-out—ready and willing. But Mullin didn't start it. Mullin doesn't do business that way. Not much! All he did was to jab his thumb over his shoulder toward the gym and say in that sneering voice: 'I'll be seein' you out there in a minute, Bunce.'

"Well, that sounded pretty good to Tim. He figured they would put on lighter gloves than usual, and Mullin would try to kill him legitimately with that right of his. That was jake with Tim. Let him try it! So Tim went into the gym and Mullin went into the cottage with Kitty.

"I was in my room while all this was happening. I heard Kitty yell. Mullin had slapped her up against the sitting room wall with the knuckles of his left hand. Tim, in the gym, heard her cry out with the pain of it. The nearest thing handy was the fast bag. Tim stepped up and began slammin' it, to get some of the red out of his system. He was giving that bag everything he had when I walked in. I was just in time to see Mullin creeping up behind him like a cat ready to spring.

"That bag was going so fast and making so much noise a horse could have walked up behind the kid, and he wouldn't have heard a sound. Mullin crept up behind him, with that steer-killing right of his all doubled up and ready to let go. I yelled. Tim said later he didn't hear me. The next thing he knew, the lights were out.

"I ran on in and I yelled at Mullin that he was a red-handed murderer, and he said: 'Well, what of it? There is an unwritten law in this State, and I killed this louse while defending the honor of my home. Phone for the dead wagon, Tobin. Get this carcass out of here.'

"Well, the kid wasn't dead, although he should have been. That blow had landed flush on the back of his head, and it should have caved in his skull. But it didn't. I got smelling salts and brandy, and in an hour I brought the kid around. Then I rushed him into the City Hospital and had X-rays taken of his head.

"The doctors said his skull must be made of reinforced concrete. There wasn't a crack or a dent in it. All the kid got out of it was a cut that they had to take a few stitches in, and a mean headache.

"But that punch finished what Mullin had started to do earlier in the week. Tim has a fight on to-night. It is his first star bout. This morning, I had him work out with Tiger Wales. Tim has entirely lost his punch. He is buffaloed. As hard as he tries, he cannot punch. If we do not snap him out of it, he will lose this fight to-night sure."

"WHO IS TIM'S opponent?" Gillian asked.

"Kid Murphy. Kid is tough, but he has nothing but a straight left. He is one of these fancy sharp-shooters. He opens you up and then shoots that left. If Tim were up to form, he would simply push that left aside and chop Kid Murphy into sausage meat. But he is in a bad way."

"Because of that blow on the back of his head?"

"No, sir. That blow did not affect him for more than a few hours. The doctors said there is absolutely no sign of concussion. Physically, Tim is as good as ever. It is all mental. Mr. Hazeltine, I have shot the works. I am up a blind alley. This is not your usual line, but you have got people out of trouble when things looked just as bad as they look now. I am not asking it as a personal favor, but as something that you owe to the ring. You are a great fight fan. I know that you and Mrs. Hazeltine never miss a good fight. Tim Bunce is the clean, modest kind of fighter that you want to see in the ring, and he is a fighter, not a lah-de-dah boxer. Will you help him out of this jam? I will do anything you say. You can see that I am very much in earnest about this."

"Yes," said Gillian, "I can see that."

He reached forward and pressed one of a row of pearl buttons at the side of his desk. The door presently opened and his secretary came in.

"A blond young man named Timothy Bunce is in the waiting room. Bring him in here."

His secretary looked at Gillian disapprovingly. He sometimes sidetracked important work when his sympathies were aroused. And she evidently suspected that he was up to his old tricks.

"Mr. Duncan is waiting to see you about that railroad fire matter," she said. "He says it is very urgent."

"Tell Mr. Duncan to drop in tomorrow," said Gillian.

His secretary frowned and hesitated. Her displeasure became more apparent. She looked at Paddy Tobin and her lips became thin.

She said coldly: "Very well, Mr. Hazeltine," and withdrew.

3

AN INVISIBLE HAND

BATTLING BUNCE WAS, as pugilists go, a good-looking youngster. He lacked the customary tokens of his profession, having neither cauliflower ears, a turnip nose, nor a bruised and swollen mouth. There were no scars visible upon his darkly tanned face, although Gillian observed an area about as large as a man's palm that had been shaved clean, at the back of his head. In the center of the shaved area was an "X" of adhesive tape holding down a wad of absorbent gauze.

His mouth was grimly closed. What particularly interested Gillian was the expression in his eyes. It was an expression of great perplexity.

The fighter's hands were in his pants pockets. He withdrew them when Paddy Tobin introduced him to Gillian. His handclasp, Gillian noted, was moist and cold and nervous. He was obviously nervous and ill at ease. Gillian knew how bashful some fighters were, once you got them out of the ring. He said calmly "Sit down, Tim."

In an effort to put the young man at his ease, he added: "I have always secretly wished that fate had sent me into the ring instead of the court room. Many times I've regretted that I had not mastered the art of sending over a good

right hook to the jaw, I would enjoy using it quite often on
crooked judges, lying witnesses, bulldozing district attor-
neys, and stupid juries. But I deal only in words—clever,
soft, hard, brutal and even, on occasion, honest. But I'd
swap all the words I know for that pair of mule hoofs you
carry in each hand!"

Battling Bunce did not smile. He looked more nervous
than ever. He sat very stiffly on the edge of his chair, with
his large brown hands firmly clasping his knees, with his
powerful chin drawn in, as a turtle draws in its head, and
with that expression of puzzlement in his clear blue eyes.

Gillian leaned forward with the smile that had won
many juries.

"Tim, Paddy has been telling me about the tough breaks
you've been having. I want you to tell me what's happened
to your punch. Put it in your own words. Why can't you
punch?"

Battling Bunce cleared his throat. Little lines of pain
appeared about his fine blue eyes.

He said huskily: "I don't know, Mr. Hazeltine. It's just
got me. I don't know."

"Try to describe it to me."

Tim hesitated.

Paddy said: "He thinks it's childish, Mr. Hazeltine."

I don't think it's anything," said the fighter, "that a lawyer
can do anything about. I think it's just a waste of your valuable time."

"Supposing," Gillian humored him, "that you tell me,
anyway."

Battling Bunce took a deep breath. The subject was obviously very painful to him.

"It's just as if somebody was holding my arm when I want to let a punch go." He looked at Gillian despairingly. Beads of sweat had appeared on his forehead, Gillian was amazed at the terrific effort it was taking Bunce to get the words out.

"Mr. Hazeltine, did you ever have one of these nightmares when you found yourself standing in the middle of a railroad track with an express train flying down the rails at you—and you couldn't move? Well," the young fellow panted, "that's what it's like. I get all set to land a punch. I time it—so. I put everything I have into it—so. But when I let the punch go, it doesn't travel. It's as if my arm was moving through molasses. Something holds it back."

Gillian said firmly: "That punch Mullin gave you yesterday must have tied up some nerve center."

But the prize fighter shook his head. "It happened before that. It happened during the middle of the week. It's just grown worse and worse."

"What we want to know," said Paddy anxiously, "is, where his punch has gone."

"WHAT," GILLIAN ASKED of Battling Bunce, "did Mullin whisper to you when you were sparring?"

"Insults!"

"About Kitty—and yourself?"

"Yes, sir."

"I should think that would have made you want to murder him."

"It did. But the harder I tried to hit, from then on, the softer my punch grew."

"Have you been boxing this morning?"

"Yes, sir."

"What luck did you have?"

"None. Absolutely none! I was boxing Tiger Wales. I hit him with everything I had. He said it was like being pelted with feathers. He said to uncork, I tried to uncork. But that thing—like a strong hand—was pulling me back. It seemed to be hanging onto my biceps, here." The blond pugilist handkerchiefed his forehead. Fresh sweat instantly stood out. "What am I going to do? Will you tell me? I'll do anything you tell me to do."

Gillian sank back and reached for a fresh cigar. He bit off the end and lighted it. He said:

"How do you feel about going in there with Kid Murphy to-night?"

"I could kill him if I was feeling right."

Paddy stared at him. "That's funny, Tim. I never heard you say a thing like that before. Did you hear him, Mr. Hazeltine? In all the time I've known him, that is the first time I ever heard him say a boasting word."

Battling Bunce lifted clenched fists from his knees.

"If I only could mean it!" he cried. "I don't believe it myself. I'm not sure of it. I'll tell you how I feel about meeting Kid Murphy to-night—I feel he is going to take me in less than two rounds!"

Gillian said gravely: "Tim, will it make you feel any better to know that I am going to take charge of all your troubles, and that I'm going to straighten everything out for you, and that somehow I am going to get Kitty back for you?"

The fighter was staring at him incredulously.

"Can you do all that?"

"If you knew Mr. Hazeltine the way I do," put in Paddy,

"you would not ask a dumb question like that. Now—are you going in there tonight and lick hell out of Murphy?"

"I—I'm going to try."

Gillian nodded. "That's a little better. Now, Tim, you run along and wait for Paddy in the reception room. I want to have a few more minutes alone with him."

When the boy was gone, Paddy opened his hands, palms up, in a futile, questioning gesture and said: "Well, you see how things stack. What is your candid opinion?"

Gillian answered: "Part of the trouble is Mullin, another part is Kitty, but the large part is—over-modesty. He had it to begin with. Why did you hold him back? Because he was too modest. A fighter should not be so modest. None of the big fighters is really modest. Convincing themselves that they are good is part of the battle. Tim Bunce is not yet convinced. In spite of his fighting ability, he has never been convinced. The loss of Kitty was a terrific blow to his pride. Mullin's tactics constituted—the knockout blow. Too much modesty! Not enough egotism! Not enough swagger!"

"How," Paddy moaned, "can we give him back his pride?"

"That would not be enough," Gillian answered. "If he is ever to reach the top of the heap he must have pride that he never before possessed. How did he explain his knock-outs?"

"He thought most of them were flukes—lucky breaks." Paddy leaned forward and his expression was imploring. "Mr. Hazeltine, I knew you would dope out what the trouble was. Now—will you take charge of things?"

Gillian looked at him dreamily. "I have had strange cases and baffling cases laid on my doorstep, but I am sure that no one ever brought me a stranger, more baffling case than this. My specialty, Paddy, is murder cases. What does a murder lawyer know about finding a punch that a prize fighter has lost?"

"This case," said Paddy gloomily, "is closer to a murder than you may guess."

It was closer to a murder than even Paddy guessed—a murder that would provide Gillian Hazeltine with one of the most amazing cases he ever took into a court room.

4

RINGSIDE

SOME RUMORS OF the broken romance of Battling Bunce had crept into the tabloids, with the result that the auditorium that night was crowded to capacity. Paddy Tobin had, on departing, left two tickets for Gillian.

"These are front row ringside, Mr. Hazeltine, and they are right next to the seats that will be used by Mullin and Kitty. I want you to look her over, and, if you have a chance, talk to her. Also, you will have a chance to see Mullin at close range."

Gillian had given his beautiful redheaded young wife a limousine for her birthday. During the ride down to the auditorium, he told her the more pertinent of the facts in the strange and baffling case of Battling Bunce. Vee Hazeltine's comments were always pungent. She said:

"I had an idea that prize fighters' souls were made of equal parts of brass and rawhide. I think it's a fascinating situation, but I am not entirely sold on your modesty theory. To me, it's much more thrilling than that. In Battling Bunce, you have a primitive man who is not reacting primitively. A hairy caveman comes along and steals his woman. Battling Bunce, also a caveman, instead of chasing him with a club studded with the fang of a sabertoothed tiger, sits and mopes and broods. Battling Bunce lost his chance to be a caveman hero in the eyes of the dewy-eyed maiden. Will he get another chance?"

"That," said her husband, "is a neat idea. I am going to work on that. But it all goes back to over-modesty, doesn't it, Vee?"

"A woman married to a lawyer learns not to argue," stated the beautiful redhead simply.

The auditorium was almost filled when they were ushered up to their seats in the first row ringside. Vee Hazeltine loved a good fight. Her color was high to-night, and her emerald-green eyes seemed greener and livelier than usual.

"Will your caveman give Kid Murphy a fight?" she wanted to know.

Gillian was waving a salute of greeting to a telegraph operator he recognized at the long bench under their edge of the ring. He said absently: "I'm afraid not."

Voices babbled about them. Smoke from cigars and cigarettes rose in a dense blue cloud.

Vee suddenly pinched Gillian's arm.

"Darling, who is that Foxy Grandpa sitting over there— pink, bald head, fringe of snow-white hair, sunburned or alcoholic nose, naughty blue eyes?"

Gillian looked. "That is Finister Chardon, the reformer."

"The one who's always in the papers?"

"Yes"—curtly. Gillian detested Finister Chardon. He was the vice president of the Greenfield National and, according to Gillian's information, a hypocrite of the first order, "His latest whiter-than-snow campaign is being launched against the brutal sport of box-fighting. Fighting is sinful! It should be banned! Ah, but note the greedy glow in his eyes. If I told you what I know about his private life, Vee, even you would blush."

"You might give my blushing machinery a test, Gill."

But Gillian was too busy nodding and waving to acquaintances.

THE RADIO ANNOUNCER, testing his microphone, grinned at Gillian, jabbed a thumb at the ring, and, with the thumb and forefinger of his other hand, gently pinched his nose. This was sign language, meaning that he expected to spend a very dull evening.

Then Josh Hammersley, of the Greenfield *Times,* sauntered up and hailed the criminal lawyer with a gladsome shout.

"What a pair of optimists you two are! Well, it all goes to flatter the power of the press. Everybody is here to-night to see the boy who had his sweetie brutally stolen from him by Champion Jake Mullin. Jake's coming, I hear."

Josh bent down and spoke in low tones into Gillian's always receptive ear.

"How are you betting on the Mullin-Walsh fight?"

"I am putting my money in municipal bonds," Gillian answered, "bursting with civic pride, as you know I am."

"It's one of these things," said Josh. "Mullin, if you want the low-down, is putting his own money on—Walsh. At three to one. He is going to lose to Walsh on a foul. There will be the usual hullabaloo—and a return match. But don't bet on that fight, Gill. What do you think of to-night's card? I hear Battling Bunce is a flash in the pan, a washout, gone absolutely stale. You will see Kid Murphy left-hand him to ribbons."

Men were moving about the ring. The announcer, in a high falsetto imitation of the inimitable Joe Humphreys, was intoning the names of the participants in the first preliminary, a four-rounder. Lightweights. Judge's decision. "In this cawna-a-ah, Billy Lewis—"

The bell presently rang. Two slim, nervous young men stopped stretching the ropes in their respective corners and came rushing out to meet in the middle of the ring in a fury of flashing gloves, of leather thudding on flesh.

The end came fifteen seconds after the bell, with the crowd on its feet roaring. Billy Lewis, exposing his chin a fraction of a second too long, went down under a left hook and stayed down.

It was the beginning of an evening of knock-outs. Two welterweights, in the second bout, kept the crowd on its feet for two rounds. Then one of the fighters went down for a count of eight, down again for a count of seven, and down, finally, for the full count.

Said Gillian to Vee: "If this keeps up, Battling Bunce may catch the spirit."

The third preliminary was stopped at the urgent request of the crowd at the beginning of the fourth round, because one of the contestants was bleeding so badly at the nose and mouth.

IMMEDIATELY AFTER THE six-round semifinal, a measure of excitement was provided for everybody by the triumphal entry of Jake Mullin.

Gillian heard him coming a long way off. His approach was comparable to the coming of a Roman emperor, dragging his captives behind his victorious chariot. At the far end of the aisle, voices began to hum. The sound grew louder and louder until it became a roar.

People stood up. Some climbed on their seats for a better view of the light heavyweight champion. The announcer, giving the items of next Saturday night's card, was ignored. Everybody was trying to see the champion. There were many boos. There were numerous hisses. There was a sprinkling of the curious birdlike sound known as "the berry." But these manifestations of the public's distaste for Jake Mullin were drowned by the prolonged roar: Hail, hail— the champion!

A police sergeant came and stood importantly beside Gillian. How the cops did love these pugs! Then, as the roar rose to full volume, a tall, broad-shouldered man with a beef-red face marked with old smallpox scars came into view, followed by a slender girl in a dark blue suit with a dark blue hat to match.

Jake Mullin, and Kitty Kelly that was—the star performers in the tragic drama of Battling Bunce!

Gillian looked quickly at the girl. She was pale and wan and woebegone. Her pale face was a mask. Her eyes were dull and lifeless. She looked forlorn. Without the explanation that Paddy Tobin had given him, Gillian would have known that here was a girl whose spirit was broken.

But there was nothing forlorn about her husband. With his hard, vain grin, he was looking about him, seeming to sop up flattery and homage as a sponge sops up water. He wore a striking tan suit, a maroon vest, and a bright green tie—grass green.

As his vain and arrogant eyes swept about, they chanced

to encounter the upturned sparkling green eyes of Mrs. Gillian Hazeltine.

The champion's grin became twisted; a smirk. It was evidently his lady-killer's smile. In the glare from the lights above the ring, Vee's face, with its bright red hair, its lovely mouth, stood out, as a beautiful face will always stand out. The champion's lower lip sagged moistly. He ran the tip of his tongue along it and said:

"Why, hullo, there, little sweetheart!"

Gillian looked from Mullin to Vee, and saw that she was meant. For a moment the famous criminal lawyer was too astounded to do anything.

"Darling," Vee said quickly, in a low voice, "please ignore him."

Upon Gillian's judicial brow a cold film of sweat formed. He went white, and his lips went gray. And in that moment was born Gillian's personal and private dislike of Champion Jake Mullin.

JOSH HAMMERSLEY PROVIDED a timely diversion. The reporter was chuckling.

"Gill," he said, "I've just heard something mighty funny. Did you know that Finister Chardon is here tonight getting local color for a red-hot interview he is going to give the boys on the evils of prize fighting?"

Gillian, still pale, nodded. "I understand that Chardon claims prize fighting is a revolting, degrading sport, and that America has a blood lust equal only to that of the old Roman mob who watched Christians served to lions. Well, Josh?"

"Well," said the reporter, "you are one of the foremost defenders of the sport, aren't you? As one of our eminent citizens, why don't you let me quote your views on the subject?"

"Not to-night," said Gillian. "I am beginning to wonder if the sport is as clean and wholesome as it's cracked up to be. I mean, judging by some of the men who are in it."

Jake Mullin was meant to overhear that, and he did. He reached up quickly and seized the reporter's wrist in fingers of iron.

"Introduce me to your swell friends, Josh."

Josh glanced at him coldly. He performed the rites with obvious reluctance. Kitty Kelly Mullin did not meet Gillian's eyes. She acknowledged the introduction with a faint nod and looked away again. Gillian did not put out his hand to Mullin. He, too, nodded faintly, but his steel-blue eyes bored into the insolent, derisive eyes of the light heavyweight champion. Mullin grinned.

"So you're Hazeltine, the crooked criminal lawyer."

"That," said Gillian, "happens to be a lie."

"And a dumb remark," put in Josh. "Good Lord, Mullin, won't you ever get any brains? Don't you realize that Mr. Hazeltine is one of the most powerful men in this city? If you had the sense of a jellyfish—"

"I got sense enough!" the champion snapped.

Josh said angrily: "Well, demonstrate it! Since you took the title away from Walker, you think you own the earth. You're so swell-headed that you don't know danger when the red light flashes in your eyes."

"Oh, ye-a-ah?" drawled the champion. "And, say, just where is the danger?"

"Never mind him," Gillian snapped, and turned to his wife: "Vee, I'm awfully sorry that you have to be present—"

Vee smiled. "Don't be sorry, darling. I love fights."

"I'm saying," persisted the reporter hotly, "that if you'll take the trouble to ask some of your racketeer friends, you'll learn that Mr. Hazeltine is a dangerous man to have for an enemy. You need a keeper, Mullin, that's what you need!"

The champion was grinning scornfully at Gillian.

"Well, let's see him get dangerous. I know he's crooked, but I want to see him act dangerous. I can act dangerous, too. Stuff that in your pipe, you two saps. I'm Jake Mullin, the light heavyweight champion of the world. Get that? I ain't afraid of any man living, and that takes in all the lawyers and ham reporters here and everywhere. And don't give me any more of your lip, Hammersley, or I'll slap you down where you belong, see?"

With that the champion turned his broad back on Josh and the Hazeltines. Vee laid a restraining hand on Gillian's arm.

"Darling, count one hundred!"

He smiled. "I'm not sore. I'm just thinking."

Said Vee: "There ought to be a law against men like him."

"There are none on the books," said Gillian. "But I am going to make some. And I am going to execute them."

The champion, in his loud voice, was talking again, this time to his woebegone wife.

"After we see what Kid Murphy does to that palooka of yours, we're goin' to do some steppin'. We're goin' to a night club—the Black Cat—to have a good time."

Gillian continued to think. He knew the proprietor of the Black Cat. It was the noisiest most expensive night club in Greenfield.

GILLIAN HEARD THE radio announcer say:

"Well, friends, the decks are now being cleared for the main bout. The contestants have not yet appeared, but the crowd is stirring with excitement. There are rumors that Battling Bunce has lost his wallop. Well, we'll see."

There were murmurs in the back of the auditorium. A lean, black-haired young man in a purple satin bathrobe came down the aisle surrounded by handlers. He climbed up and ducked through the ropes. There was faint cheering. It persisted as a man came down another aisle, a blond young man in a blue flannel bathrobe. Behind him, pale and worried, came Paddy Tobin and two men in shirt sleeves.

"There," said Gillian, "is the boy who lost his punch."

The referee was bending over the ropes, beckoning to Jake Mullin.

The radio announcer was saying: "The two contestants in the star bout of the evening are in the ring now, folks. Can you hear me above the roaring? The crowd isn't roaring for Murphy or Bunce. It's roaring for the light heavyweight champion, Jake Mullin. He's been asked up into the ring. One of these boys—Bunce—has been Mullin's sparring partner. The winner of to-night's bout may meet Mullin some time in the not distant future.

"Can you hear me above the yelling? The champion is being introduced to the crowd. Now he's clasping his hands above his head and making little ducking bows, in the immemorial manner. The two boys are still in their bathrobes. Murphy looks good, folks. He looks mighty good. His condition looks excellent. But Bunce looks dazed. There's a queer look in his eyes. Something is certainly the matter with Bunce.

"Mullin is climbing out of the ring now, folks. He shook hands with Murphy, and it looked as if he was wishing him luck. But he absolutely ignored Battling Bunce. There must be something in these rumors that are going around that there was some unpleasantness between the two men at the training camp. Hey, Jake! Hey—*Jake!* Won't you say a few words to the radio audience?"

Mullin had climbed down and was grasping the mike.

"Good evenin', folks. This is Jake Mullin, the light heavy-weight champion. I dropped in here to-night to look over the boys in the star bout. If I was betting I'd put my money on Kid Murphy. I just want to say to you folks that you can count on me to give all my friends a good showing on the Fourth of July. I am in the pink of condition. I expect to take Frankie Walsh in one round."

The radio announcer recaptured the microphone and said, ironically: "I'll hire some violets to do the blushing for you, Jake." And into the microphone:

"Well, friends, there's a lot of tension around here now. You could cut it with a knife. The two boys have taken off their bathrobes. They have brand-new gloves on. The referee has told them to give us a good fight and to break clean and so forth. They are in their corners waiting for the bell. Battling Bunce is right above me. Physically, he looks perfect, but he still acts strange. Kid Murphy is on his tiptoes, nervous as a cat, as he always is before a fight starts. They are quite a contrast. The Battler is a blond, sunburned to the color of an old saddle, and he has as beautiful a pair of shoulders as you ever saw. Kid Murphy is a brunette. You might almost call him a hot-house brunette. He has black hair, black or dark brown eyes, and his skin is as white as a gardenia. He has square shoulders. His build is bony. The crowd is buzzing with anticipation and—"

Clang!

AS THE BELL rang, Gillian distinctly heard Paddy Tobin say to Battling Bunce:

"Watch out for that left. Tie him up. Get under it and go after his stomach. Pound it pink, then work on his jaw."

"With what?" grunted Jake Mullin loudly.

Battling Bunce pushed himself away from the ropes with an air of resignation. His subsequent actions were those of an automaton. Kid Murphy came springily out from his corner, with his famous left extended, his right dancing up and down under his chin, ready to dart in like a snake or to block blows to his notoriously delicate midsection. One sport writer had said of Kid Murphy: "The Kid has an iron jaw—but a custard stomach. His Achilles heel is down where the vest begins."

The two men met approximately in ring center to exchange a volley of unimportant punches. They fell into a clinch, which the referee broke by walking between them. Battling Bunce launched a right to the midsection, which Murphy blocked. And Bunce blocked with his elbow a left jab to the head. They clinched again, and again the referee interfered.

Murphy began to lead, and Bunce to fall back. It was soon evident that Murphy was carrying the fight. Bunce backed off and backed off. The crowd began to hoot. Some one jeered: "Get in there and fight, you big slob!" Some one else made the usual sarcastic reference to roller skates.

Gillian knew that Battling Bunce was trying. His shoulders and face were already agleam with sweat. He was trying, but that invisible force was holding back his punches.

The round ended decisively in Kid Murphy's favor. Paddy Tobin threw a bucketful of cold water into Battling Bunce's face, and Gillian heard him exhorting him:

"What did I tell you, Tim? He hasn't a thing but that left. Go in there this round and take him. Open up, will you?"

"Sure, sure," said Bunce, "I'll open up. I'll take him this round."

"He's as bad," pronounced Vee, "as either of those lightweights in that first preliminary."

"Worse, sweetie; much worse," said Jake Mullin. And Gillian breathed hard. Something was going to happen to Jake Mullin. Gillian was not yet certain what it would be, but it would be—sufficient.

When the bell rang for the second round, Battling Bunce leaped out as though he really meant business. Kid Murphy met him with that left of his straight out. Bunce brought his glove slashing down on the triceps; the arm gave way.

It happened in a space of time measurable only by a split-second watch. Kid Murphy slipped on a wet spot on the canvas. To balance himself he threw his right arm wildly backward. For at least three seconds his stomach was utterly unprotected. Bunce closed in. He drove one fist and then the other into that ready target.

And nothing happened! The crowd was roaring. Having had their appetite for knock-outs well whetted, they wanted another one.

"Finish it up!"

"Kill him, Battler!"

"Chop him down!"

But Kid Murphy had not even staggered. A grin flitted over his lips. He knew that the rumors he had been hearing were true. Battling Bunce had entered the ring without his famous punch! Battling Bunce had had his chance to send over two knock-out punches. He had tried—and failed.

KID MURPHY'S DEFENSE became noticeably careless as he tried for a knock-out. Gillian saw the sweat, a shining layer of it, rolling down Bunce's magnificent body. The boy was trying. For a long time Gillian wondered what it was that Bunce reminded him of. And suddenly he realized: a slow motion picture. He moved as if he were handicapped by some medium much thicker than air. Bunce himself had compared it to molasses. He was clumsy and slow.

Once Kid Murphy dropped his guard and beckoned with his gloves. The gesture said: "Come on and hit me. I dare you to hit me!" He left himself wide open, and Bunce tried to hit him, but could not.

"How," Gillian moaned, "can I convince a fighter who has lost his punch that he has one of the greatest punches in ring history?"

And Vee said grimly: "You must do something for that boy, Gill. It's tragic—simply tragic."

Gillian heard Mullin say to Kitty with a chuckle: "Well, baby, what do you think of your hee-ro now? So that is the beautiful boy you were betting your sugar on, is it?"

And Kitty Kelly answered him in a fierce little voice:

"I'm still betting on him!"

Gillian looked at her as the bell rang for the third round. He had reached the conclusion that there was only one way to help Battling Bunce. He must make him angry. And to make him angry, he must secure some information from Kitty Kelly.

Battling Bunce looked tired. He came heavily off his stool. He seemed to stagger a little as he went out to meet his opponent. Kid Murphy rushed out and drove him into a corner. With a right hook to the jaw; he spun Bunce around. Then he let drive with his left at the back of Bunce's head.

A sympathetic pang throbbed for a moment in the back of Gillian's head. He was certain that that blow had landed on the "X" of adhesive tape. But it was not a rabbit punch. It was legal.

Bunce went down under it. His legs collapsed. He fell on his left side and rolled over limply on his back, with one glove thrown over his face.

It had happened so quickly that the crowd was unprepared. But the crowd was on its feet now, baying.

Kid Murphy retired to the farthest corner, draped his arms along the ropes and tried to look nonchalant. He could not repress a grin. He had never expected to win this fight. The best he had hoped for was a draw.

The referee's hand rose and fell over Battling Bunce. The fighter's face, partly visible under the protecting glove, was turned toward Gillian. The boy's eyes were partly open. He was looking at Kitty Kelly. His mouth was working. He was, Gillian was certain, conscious. Gillian swallowed uncomfortably.

Paddy crawled through the ropes and helped Tim Bunce to his feet. The fighter walked unsteadily across the ring and congratulated his victor.

Jake Mullin sprang up and made his way through the crowd to Kid Murphy's corner. And thus the opportunity was given to Gillian for a word with Kitty Kelly.

He said rapidly: "Mrs. Mullin, I am trying to find some way of helping Tim Bunce. I need your help."

She gazed at him levelly.

"Paddy told me Tim was going to you. How can I help?"

And Gillian said: "I want to get Tim mad. I want to get him fighting mad. Is there any way?"

"There might be, Mr. Hazeltine. But I don't know. He seems to have lost all heart… You might call him dishonest. Call him a crook. Very few people know it, but Tim's father died in the penitentiary. Tim insists that his father was framed on a burglary charge. Whether that is true or not, Tim has always been terribly touchy on the subject of honesty."

"I'll try it," said Gillian.

She touched his arm. "I'll do anything you ask, to help Tim get straightened out again. I—I failed him." Her eyes filled with tears.

Gillian turned a gentle smile on Vee and said: "Darling, I am going to park you for a few minutes in the car. I have something to say to Bunce."

5

THE BEST-LAID PLANS—

WHEN GILLIAN ENTERED the dressing room, Battling Bunce was stretched out on the rubbing table. To Paddy Tobin, Gillian whispered:

"No matter what I say to Tim, back me up. Understand? There's no time now for explanations."

Paddy nodded. And Gillian said, in an explosive voice: "Bunce, why did you throw that fight to-night?"

The fighter turned his head and looked at him with amazement.

"That story of your lost punch," Gillian angrily went on, "was so clever that it fooled me. And I'm an expert in dealing with liars!"

Battling Bunce sat up and swung his legs over the side of the table. He stared at Gillian. Huskily he said:

"What are you saying, Mr. Hazeltine?"

"I'm saying," Gillian rapped out, "that that fight was fixed. You sold out to Murphy. You didn't lose your punch; you sold it!"

"That's a damned lie! Who said I sold out?"

"Bluffing again!" Gillian jeered. "I told you this morning I won't help any man who won't come clean with me. You lied to me."

"Is that so, Mr. Hazeltine?" Paddy gasped.

"You bet it's so! This fine two-fisted fighter of yours has been doublecrossing you. He's been lying to both of us."

Tim repeated: "That's a damned lie and you know it!"

"Listen to him!" Gillian snapped. "All I have to say is that any man who sells out as you did deserves to lose his girl!"

Tim was flexing and unflexing his taped hands. His great chest was rising and falling with the labor of his indignation.

"Look here!" he panted. "Maybe I put on a lousy show in there tonight, but I'm not crooked. I didn't lie. I didn't sell out. If you call me a crook again I'm going to knock you down." His face was flushed and his eyes were blazing. Gillian wanted to cheer, but he said:

"You're as crooked as your father was. You would knock me down, would you? Why don't you knock down the man who put the label on you? You don't dare knock him down!"

"I'd knock Gene Tunney down for calling me crooked! I'd knock Jack Dempsey down for calling me crooked! I never threw a fight in my life. You can call me anything you want, and maybe it's true, but no man alive is going to call me a crook! Ask Paddy!"

Paddy arose promptly to the occasion. He did not know where this amazing conversation was leading. But he trusted Gillian.

"How do I know you're on the up-and-up?" he growled. "Maybe you did sell out to Kid Murphy to-night. How do I know?"

"You're a pair of skunks!" Battling Bunce raged. He looked dangerous. Gillian began to wonder how much further this taunting might go, if he had any regard for his personal safety. The trick had worked. The problem now was to keep Battling Bunce mad long enough for the important mission Gillian had in mind to be executed.

"No wonder your Kitty is ashamed and disgusted! All her faith in you is gone. She was for you up to the moment she learned that you had sold out."

THE BATTLER ROARED: "Who said I sold out? Tell me that! Tell me who said I sold out to Murphy!"

"Jake Mullin," said Gillian.

"He did, did he?"

"I heard him telling that to a lot of people. He said all this talk of your losing your punch was so much boloney. He said he could produce several witnesses to prove you had lain down to Murphy for a thousand dollars."

"He's a damned liar!"

"Yes?" drawled Gillian. "Why don't you tell him so? You're so anxious to knock somebody down. Knock him down. You don't dare knock him down! You don't dare to call him a liar to his face, and knock him down!"

"I don't, don't I?"

"No, you don't," Paddy sneered. "It's just as I thought. Nothin' but a pack of lies. You dirty little crook, you! After all I've done for you—selling out right under my nose! Believe me, Bunce, I'm washed up with you."

"I'll show you," the fighter panted, "and I'll show Mullin whether I'm crooked or not. Where is he?"

"Is this more embroidery?" Gillian asked of Paddy.

"Where is he?" Bunce roared. "I'll show you whether it's embroidery!"

"You mean," Gillian marveled, "you'll walk up to Mullin and hit him right in the jaw with everything you've got?"

"All I ask is, where is he?"

"Will you hit him as you've never hit any man before?"

"I sure will!"

"What with?" Paddy snorted.

"This!" shouted Battling Bunce, and he lifted his huge taped right fist to a level with Gillian's nose.

"I think you're bluffing," said Gillian.

"So do I," said Paddy. "I think all you want is the chance to get out of here and hide your face with shame!"

"Where is Mullin?" the fighter demanded.

"At the Black Cat," said Gillian. "It's a night club. It's in the middle of the block on Maplewood, between—"

"I know where it is. Where are my clothes?"

"Here," said Paddy. "And let me tell you something, big boy. If you don't knock Mullin cock-eyed, we'll know you're a crook."

"Leave that to me," said Tim grimly. He was already hurrying into his clothes. When he was gone, Paddy said to Gillian:

"I wish you'd had that idea before the fight, Mr. Hazel-tine. What good do you figure it will do now?"

"If he knocks Mullin down, it will prove to him that he still has his punch, won't it?"

"Yes, sir; but by to-morrow morning he will say what he always says—it was nothing but an accident. That blamed modesty will be riding him again. How are you going to get around that?"

"Let to-morrow morning," Gillian answered, "take care of that. You have retained me to convince Tim Bunce that he has one of the most terrific punches ever seen in a ring. With my own peculiar methods, I will convince him."

"Who killed him?" Gillian snapped

"But suppose something goes wrong, Mr. Hazeltine? Suppose Tim cools off and loses his punch again before he finds Mullin! Suppose Mullin, if Tim does find him, beats him to the punch? Suppose waiters or bouncers or friends of Mullin break up the argument before Tim has a chance to hit Mullin? Worst of all, suppose Tim is pinched for disorderly conduct?"

"I was just coming to that," said the lawyer. "Part of my plan is that Tim must be arrested and booked for felonious assault, or at least disorderly conduct. That, in fact, is your job. You are to follow Tim to the Black Cat. You are to pick up a cop you do not know on the way. Tell him that Jake Mullin is going to be feloniously assaulted by Tim Bunce. If the policeman hesitates, remind him that here is an excellent chance to grab off some publicity. Cops love publicity. Tim has undoubtedly taken a taxi. Follow him in one. Pick up the cop. When Bunce is locked up, telephone me at my house. Say nothing to reporters. As Tim's attorney, I will do all the talking."

Paddy Tobin reached for his hat and hurried out.

GILLIAN HAZELTINE RETURNED to the main entrance of the auditorium. Most of the crowd was gone, but among the loiterers he found Finister Chardon, the reformer. Chardon was talking to a semicircle of bored and gloomy newspaper men.

The criminal lawyer paused and watched the scene. Finister Chardon had succumbed not long ago to what Gillian callously called Front Page Itch. The greedy-eyed little man had discovered how easy it was, by attacking this civic evil and that public nuisance, to find his name springing out at him from the front pages of the newspapers.

Gillian believed that few reformers were sincere or honest. It was his private belief that they were all hypocrites and that they had an insensate greed for publicity. He knew many things about this whited sepulchre of a Chardon.

He listened to Finister Chardon now. The reformer was saying, in an oratorical manner:

"All of you gentlemen saw what I saw to-night—a series of revolting spectacles; men springing at each other like beasts, to pummel and pound each other, to attempt, if possible, to batter each other into insensibility. You saw blood spilled. You saw men struck down as if they were swine in a stock-yard. I say, gentlemen, and I say it with all the indignation of a decent man aroused, that this so-called 'sport' of prize fighting is degrading and harmful and vicious."

He paused and Gillian reflected that nothing that Finister Chardon was saying was new. Simply because Finister Chardon was one of the city's wealthiest and most power-ful citizens, it happened to be news. The publicity-loving banker went on:

"Gentlemen, I have never attended a prize fight before. I came to-night with an open mind. Sport, if deserving, should be encouraged. I was anxious to know whether prize fighting was a fit spectacle for my daughter and my son to watch. If so, I would lend it my hearty support. But what happened? My blood turned cold at those specta-cles of savagery I witnessed. You can quote me as saying emphatically that prize fighting is the most demoralizing influence in this country to-day. That is all I have to say."

Josh Hammersley was one of the reporters. There was upon his face the look of a man who has eaten some-thing that is not comfortably digesting. He saw Gillian and winked. Strolling over to the lawyer, he said:

"Gill, can't something be done about this old reptile? All of this hooey he has been spilling must go on the front page. I wish my paper had the courage to print in a paral-lel column some of the facts of his private life—the lousy old hypocrite!"

Gillian grinned and said: "I thought the press was free."

Josh snorted and went out. He had to catch the last edition with the interview.

The reformer waited until the last of the reporters had asked his last perfunctory question. Then he strolled over to Gillian.

"Mr. Hazeltine," he said solemnly, "I must say that I was astonished to see you at the very ringside to-night with your charming wife. It seems to me that men of your standing in this community should set an example to the youth of Greenfield. What a revolting spectacle it was!"

Gillian glanced at his watch. It was eleven twenty. Battling Bunce would soon reach the Black Cat. Paddy Tobin would arrive there a few minutes later.

"IF YOU ARE asking for my opinion," said Gillian, "there are evils in this community which are much more deserving of your attention than prize fighting. The night clubs."

Finister Chardon looked at him.

"The night clubs?" he repeated.

"They are," said Gillian, "like cancers gnawing at the very civic heart of Greenfield. You should see them with your own eyes, Mr. Chardon. You should see young girls wearing not enough clothing to cover them decently."

He paused and watched the results. A brighter gleam had come into the reformer's greedy little blue eyes.

"These girls, hardly more than children," Gillian went on, "dance in nothing more than chiffon. It is deplorable. Why not see one of these places for yourself? Draw your own conclusions."

Again he paused. Still brighter gleamed the reformer's little eyes. And Gillian knew that Finister Chardon was snared. Finister Chardon was seeing his name once again on the front pages, this time denouncing those sinks of iniquity known as the night clubs. It was Gillian's intention that Finister Chardon should see his name on the front pages in still another connection.

"My car is outside, Mr. Chardon. I will be delighted to drop you off at the Black Cat. You need no introduction there, no card of admission."

"I consider it my civic duty," said Finister Chardon, "to

go to the Black Cat. But I won't trouble you, Mr. Hazeltine. I have my own car."

Gillian said good night to him and walked out to Vee's limousine. When they reached home, Gillian went at once to his study to await Paddy Tobin's telephone call. He seated himself at his desk and lighted a cigar. The hands of the little gold clock at the back of his desk moved to midnight and on to half-past twelve.

Gillian grew uneasy. If his plans had miscarried, he was certain that Tim Bunce would be beyond human help.

At twelve forty, Gillian heard the silvery tinkling of the back-door bell. He sat up alertly. That doorbell at this time of night invariably meant trouble. It was said that the underworld had beaten a path to the Hazeltine back door, but this was not literally true. There were invisible trails leading off, fanwise, from the back door through meadows and woodlots. Down these trails came men in trouble— after midnight.

The bell rang again. Gillian's Japanese houseman, Toro, was evidently sleeping soundly. The lawyer descended the back stairs into the kitchen. He unlocked the door, threw it open and peered into the night.

Paddy Tobin sagged against the doorjamb. His eyes were half-closed. The little Irishman was breathless. Great drops of sweat were running down his face.

Gillian took him by the arm, pulled him in and sat him down in a chair. Paddy's eyes rolled from side to side. He placed his hand over his heart and gasped:

"Just—a—minute."

Gillian waited. Paddy nipped his lower lip between his teeth.

"I—ran all the way. Mullin—is dead!"

"Who killed him?" Gillian snapped.

"Tim Bunce!"

"With what?"

"A right uppercut to the jaw!"

GILLIAN WENT INTO the dining room. When he returned with a bottle of Scotch and two tall, pale green glasses, Paddy stared at him broodingly. Gillian placed the glasses on the white-enameled kitchen table and opened the electric refrigerator. He put ice cubes into the glasses and uncapped a bottle of White Rock and mixed two stiff highballs.

Paddy Tobin disposed of his in gulps. He put the empty glass down and struck the table with his fist.

"Mr. Hazeltine, it's up to you. Unless you do something about it, Tim will go to the electric chair. And I doubt if there's anything you or any other lawyer can do about it. It was first degree murder!"

Gillian said calmly; "Tell me what happened."

Paddy began to talk rapidly, in a thin, excited voice.

"I did just what you told me to do. I went down to the Black Cat. I stopped at the corner of Maplewood and Wayne to pick up a cop. I told him what you told me. I told him that Tim was on his way to the Black Cat to attack Jake Mullin.

"When the cop and I went in, Tim was sitting at a table over against the wall watching the door. If he recognized me, he didn't show it. The cop and I waited by the checkroom for ten minutes. A lot of people came in before Mullin did."

"Did Finister Chardon come in?"

"Yes, sir. Right after he came in, Mullin blew along with Tiger Wales and Micky Welsh."

"Was Kitty with them?"

"No, sir. The head waiter took them to a table near the dance floor. Before they could sit down, Tim was over there. He knocked over two tables on his way over. There was an awful lot of excitement. A couple of women yelled, but I could hear Tim even above all the racket. He said, 'Call me a crook to my face, you rat!' And it happened before anybody could do anything. In all the fights I ever watched, I never saw a blow like it. Do you remember the way Dempsey kept hitting Firpo in the second round? It was something like those punches, only it had more back of it.

"Even above the yelling and shouting, you could hear the crack of his fist on Mullin's jawbone. It was a terrible sound, Mr. Hazeltine. And it all happened so quick that nobody had time to do anything. Mike Flaherty, the cop, started from the checkroom window the minute Tim started from his table. By the time he reached Mullin's table, Mullin was lying there on the floor, as dead as a carload of bacon."

Paddy Tobin paused and picked up the fresh highball Gillian had mixed for him.

He went on:

"The cop grabbed Tim by one arm, and I grabbed him by the other."

Gillian snapped: "What did you say to him?"

"I told him to keep his mouth shut; that you would do the talking."

"Good," Gillian approved.

"I stayed right with him, Mr. Hazeltine. Flaherty, the

cop, took him down to the Fourth Precinct jail in a taxicab, and I went along. He's down there now. And they've got him booked for murder."

Gillian was lighting a fresh cigar with steady hands. Paddy stared at him imploringly.

"MR. HAZELTINE, YOU'VE got men out of tight corners before, but what chance has Tim got? It was premeditated murder," Paddy moaned.

"No," said Gillian, "it was premeditated assault."

"What difference does it make? Won't that cop testify on the stand that I picked him up and took him there because Tim was going to assault Mullin? Won't there be a hundred witnesses who saw Tim go up and wallop Mullin in the jaw?"

"Yes," Gillian said.

"Didn't you get Tim into this?" Paddy cried.

"I did."

"Are you going to stand behind him? Are you going to go into court with him?"

"I am," said Gillian.

"But even if you can get him off—and how in hell can you possibly save him from the chair—even if you do, the boy's life is ruined."

"It was," Gillian pointed out, "ruined before he killed Mullin. You retained me to get his punch back, didn't you? I got it back, didn't I?"

Paddy groaned.

Gillian pressed a button set into the wall near the back door. He said to Paddy:

"My chauffeur will take you home, Paddy. I can't tell you to go to bed and stop worrying. I admit that this is one of the toughest cases I have ever undertaken, and I admit that things look pretty black.

"But there are ways, Paddy. I'll do my best."

"Yes, sir; I know you will," said Paddy.

But there was no confidence in his tones. His eyes still were terrified, and behind that terrified look, Gillian knew, was a picture of Tim Bunce being strapped into the electric chair.

When Paddy was gone, Gillian returned to his study. He opened a new box of cigars, placed his feet on the desk and began to smoke. The first gray of dawn at the window found him still sitting there, his attitude unchanged, his face gray and tired. But the sixteenth cigar had given him an idea.

6

CHARGED WITH MURDER

THE OCCUPANT OF Cell No. 47 was a thoroughly defeated young man. When Gillian, that next morning, stopped midway down the long corridor and looked in, Tim Bunce was seated on the side of his cot with his elbows on his knees and his chin in his hands. His eyes looked burned out.

Said Gillian: "Tim, I want to congratulate you. That was a wonderful punch."

The fighter stared at him blankly, then he slowly stood up and came to the door.

"Are you trying to be funny?" he growled.

Gillian gave him a look of surprise. "Funny?" he repeated. "I don't think it's funny. I think it's wonderful. Last night you couldn't hit Kid Murphy hard enough to make him blink. A half hour later, you delivered one of the most terrific punches in the history of prize fighting. Your punch came back!"

"No, it didn't," the young man disagreed. "I happened to hit him just so. It wasn't much of a punch. It was an accident."

"Tim," said Gillian, "won't anything convince you that you have one of the greatest punches in ring history?"

"It was an accident," Tim insisted. "And it's going to send me to the chair. Well, let them send me to the chair. I don't care."

"I do," said Gillian.

"Well, I don't. What have I got to live for?"

"Kitty's free now."

"What of it? Do you suppose she would be interested in a murderer?"

"Girls have stood by men through worse troubles than this. Look here, Tim. Don't you want to get out of this jam, and marry Kitty, and go back to the ring and become famous and successful?"

"What chance is there?" demanded that over-modest young man.

"I'm going to do my best," Gillian promised. "They'll take you into the homicide court in a few minutes. I will meet you there. The plea will be not guilty. Later, you will appear before the Grand Jury. Have reporters been in here this morning?"

"Yes, sir."

"What did you tell them?"

"Nothing. I referred them to you."

"Keep on referring them to me. I will do all of your talking."

Battling Bunce said sullenly: "Oh, what's the use? It's all a waste of time."

Gillian turned and walked away. He was furious. How could he untangle one of the greatest punches in ring history from the shyest, most modest nature he had ever encountered? How could he convince this lion that he was not a lamb?

Gillian's humor was not improved when, as he was descending the jail steps, he saw the district attorney climbing out of his coupé at the curb. Between Gillian and the district attorney there existed—and had existed for years—the heartiest enmity.

Adelbert Yistle was a square-built man, with a strong judicial forehead surmounted by a mop of iron-gray hair, and a massive pair of jaws surmounted by an iron-gray mustache. Mr. Yistle was a commanding figure. He was extremely ambitious, and hoped some day to become governor of the State.

THE DISTRICT ATTORNEY'S mouth tightened when he saw Gillian.

He said bluntly:

"Is it true, Gillian, that you are going to defend this prize fighter who murdered Jake Mullin?"

Gillian looked at him coldly and nodded. "Yes, Bert."

"That means, I suppose," the district attorney said testily, "that we are going to have another court room circus."

"Perhaps," Gillian agreed with a hard grin, "it does."

"A hundred witnesses saw Bunce strike Mullin down in cold blood. It was premeditated murder. And I'll bet a dollar to a plugged nickel that you're going into court with a plea of not guilty and a line-up of trick witnesses."

"On the contrary," said Gillian, "I am convinced that Bunce is guilty as hell."

"Then why are you taking his defence?"

"Some one," Gillian murmured, "must defend the under-dog."

The district attorney's expression became even more grim.

"You know damned well that the calendar is crowded. You're going into court with some kind of three-ring circus. Damn it, I can tell it by the look in your eye! You don't care how congested the courts are! You don't care how long really important cases are held back! No! You'll take my time, and judges' time, and valuable court room time, to put on your clowning act!"

"Thank you, Bert," said Gillian dryly, "for the suggestion."

"You won't," Mr. Yistle stated angrily, "find much sympathy in any court room in this town. You might as well save your trickery. It won't work. I am going to send this Battling Bunce to the chair, and all your foxiness won't stop me!"

"You will have to admit," said Gillian, "that that was a wonderful punch. A terrific punch! It may go down in history as the most terrific punch ever landed by one pugilist on the jaw of another."

"It will, if I have anything to say about it!" snapped the district attorney.

"Thank you, Bert," Gillian said. "I wanted to make sure that we agreed on that."

He went on down the steps, leaving Mr. Yistle standing there, staring after him with an expression of chagrin and puzzlement.

It was only fair for Mr. Yistle to assume that Gillian was up to his old tricks. He was going into a court room with something else in his mind other than pure justice.

That morning he stood beside Battling Bunce in homicide court and entered a plea of not guilty to murder. Later, he stood beside that lamblike lion when he was called before the Grand Jury. The Grand Jury hearkened intelligently to a mass of carefully prepared evidence and remanded Timothy Bunce, murderer, to the court of Special Sessions, then sitting.

The newspapers had become tremendously interested in the case. The pertinent facts in the love triangle of Kitty Kelly, Jake Mullin, and Tim Bunce were excavated from various sources and paraded upon the front pages. The murder was referred to by the tabloids as a "Passion Crime." Startling court room disclosures were promised.

Finister Chardon, the reformer, seized upon this golden opportunity to ventilate his views upon the revolting sport of prize fighting.

Then, suddenly, mysteriously, his name vanished from the front pages. It was as if he had opened his mouth to utter still louder denunciations when he discovered a fishbone sticking in his throat.

Who put that fishbone there? Who had suddenly obstructed that flow of oratory?

7

THE TRIAL OPENS

EVERYBODY IN THE court room stood up as Judge Barlow took his place on the bench. He was a slender, scholarly-looking man, with a long, narrow face, a high forehead and a very sensitive mouth. He nodded to a bailiff and the bailiff droned:

"Oyez! Oyez! Oyez! The Superior Court within and for Greenfield County, criminal term, is open and in session at this place. All persons having cause or action who are summoned to appear herein will give attention according to the law."

Judge Barlow said: "You may call the jury," and a sheriff hastened to obey him. And presently twelve good men and true filed in and took their places in the jury box. The clerk now read the charge. On its completion, Gillian Hazeltine arose and said "The defendant pleads not guilty."

Mr. Yistle and his assistant, Mr. Bullock, looked at Gillian narrowly, as though they expected to see him produce a rabbit from a silk hat. Gillian sat down beside the defendant and the trial began.

In his opening address to the jury, Mr. Yistle stated simply that he would endeavor to prove that the accused was guilty of a crime which, according to the statutes, would leave the jury no alternative but to send Timothy Bunce to the electric chair.

"I will prove to you gentlemen, by the testimony of credible witnesses, that the accused did, with premeditation and deliberation and forethought, bring about the death of Jake Mullin, thereby making him guilty of the crime of murder in the first degree. Will Dr. Cutler take the stand?"

Dr. Cutler was the coroner of Greenfield. A middle-aged man with a clipped gray mustache and an air of great self-possession, Dr. Cutler made an excellent witness. He answered questions crisply and without hesitation.

Mr. Bullock examined him for the prosecution.

"Dr. Cutler, on the night of June 20 were you called to a night club on Maplewood Avenue to make an examination of the body of a man who had been killed there—the Black Cat Club, to be exact?"

"Yes, sir."

"Did you ascertain the identity of this corpse?"

"Yes, sir. The dead man was Jake Mullin, the light heavyweight champion."

"Kindly describe to the jury how Jake Mullin had been killed."

"He was struck forcibly in the jaw. The jaw was fractured. The force of the blow traveling backward along the jawbone ruptured a ligament connecting the base of the skull to the Atlas, or the first upper bone of the spinal column. This, in turn, caused a hemorrhage in the spinal cord, resulting in almost instant death."

"Thank you, Doctor; that will be all. Does the defence wish to cross-examine?"

GILLIAN STOOD UP with a smile.

"Doctor," he said, "in all the years of your experience, have you ever known of a death that was brought about in quite this fashion; that is to say, the death of a strong man?"

"No, Mr. Hazeltine; I have not."

"In the course of your examination of the *corpus delicti*, did you have cause to note the muscular and bony development in the neck, face and shoulders?"

"I did, sir."

"Were you impressed with the unusual strength of bone and muscular tissue in the dead man's neck, shoulders and so forth?"

"Yes, sir."

"This man's muscles were developed far above those of the average man, were they not?"

"They were indeed, Mr. Hazeltine, Jake Mullin was a tremendously powerful specimen. His muscles were like ropes. And he had particularly heavy bones."

"You would say, would you not, that to cause such a man's death, a blow on the jaw must have been more than an ordinary blow. Would you not say that it must have been almost a superhuman blow?"

"It was a terrific blow," the coroner agreed.

Mr. Yistle stirred. So did Mr. Bullock. The district attorney said to his assistant: "Do you suppose that Hazeltine is planning to prove that some other man struck that blow?"

And his assistant, an incurable yes-man, answered: "The very same thought had occurred to me, Mr. Yistle."

"Now, Doctor," Gillian was saying, "you have, now and then, examined the contestants in prize fights, have you not?"

"Yes, sir; I have."

"You have, then, been in a position to study closely and professionally the results of knock-out blows to the jaw. In your experience, Doctor, have you ever seen results comparable to those which resulted from the blow with which the defendant struck Jake Mullin?"

"No, Mr. Hazeltine; never."

"It would be almost impossible to exaggerate the terrific power of that blow which fractured a jawbone, tore off a ligament and created a hemorrhage in the spinal cord?"

"It was," the doctor agreed emphatically, "a mighty blow."

"Now, Doctor," Gillian went on, "have you ever examined a man killed by the kick of a horse—specifically, the kick of a horse in the jaw?"

"Yes, sir; I once performed an autopsy on such a man."

"Will you tell me whether or not the results of that horse's kick and the uppercut that killed Jake Mullin were similar?"

"They were almost identical. In each case, the jawbone was fractured, the ligament was torn and the cord was ruptured."

"So that you would say, would you, Doctor, that the defendant's punch was almost, or exactly, the equivalent of the blow delivered by the hind hoof of a killing horse?"

The doctor was smiling. "It could be expressed that way. Yes, sir."

Mr. Yistle arose majestically to his feet. "Your honor," he said irritably, "I beg that you request my honorable adversary to refrain from indulging in his circus tricks. These questions and answers are utterly irrelevant. The coroner, we all know, is called to the stand merely to establish for legal purposes the identity of the *corpus delicti* and to describe the manner whereby his death was brought about."

Gillian bowed to Mr. Yistle and again to the bench.

"Your honor, I withdraw any questions which Mr. Yistle takes exception to. I am through with this witness."

HE SAT DOWN. There was a puzzled look in Battling Bunce's eyes.

"It was a wonderful punch, Tim," Gillian whispered to him.

"It was an accident," Tim insisted.

"I will convince you yet," Gillian promised. "It was like the kick of a horse. It was a terrific punch."

"It wasn't, but even if it was, all these questions of yours make me look guiltier than ever."

Gillian dismissed his objection with a careless flip of the hand. "We will get around to that in due time, Tim. The main point is: what a wonderful punch that was!"

The next witness called by the State was Tiger Wales, a colored man. His resemblance to Jack Johnson, of fistic fame, was pronounced. With perfect poise, the black man took the stand. His grin was infectious. Half the crowd began to smile.

Duly sworn, he testified, under rapid questions, that he was a heavyweight prize fighter, and that he had entered the Black Cat Club with the murdered man and Micky Welsh, a welterweight fighter, at approximately 11.45 P.M.

"Will you kindly describe to the jury what happened?"

"Yas, suh. We-all went over to a table an' jes' when we wuz settin' down, there was this ruckus behind us. First thing Ah knowed, this Battlin' Bunce came a chargin' up to Mr. Mullin and he says, 'Call me a crook to my face, will you?' An' befo' Mr. Mullin could do a thing—*wham!* Dassall."

The colored fighter relaxed with his beatific grin and the court room roared.

When order had been restored, Mr. Yistle frowningly requested the witness to elaborate on that word *"Wham."*

"Just what do you mean by wham? Who whammed whom?"

" 'At white boy yonder—he whammed Mr. Mullin."

"With what?"

"With the purtiest right uppercut Ah ever laid mah eyes on, suh."

"I see. Did Mr. Mullin say anything to him prior to his striking that blow?"

"No, suh; Mr. Mullin didn' hab time to say nuffin'."

"The defendant simply rushed up to him and—"

"Wham!" said the witness.

"You are certain, are you, Tiger, that Mr. Mullin did not strike the first blow, and that he said absolutely nothing calculated to provoke the defendant to anger?"

The black man blinked. "Says which?"

Judge Barlow leaned forward. "He means, Tiger, did Mr. Mullin say anything to Battling Bunce that might have made Bunce angry enough to strike him?"

"No, Jedge; he didn't say nuffin', and he didn't do nuffin'. He didn't have no time. It happened jes' lak I said. There was Mr. Mullin. Up comes Mr. Bunce. *Wham!* Good-by, Mr. Mullin! Dassall."

Mr. Yistle sat down. Gillian stood up. He walked over to the witness.

"Tiger," said Gillian, "you have done a fair amount of whamming in your own time, have you not?"

"Yas, suh," agreed the grinning black man. "Ah've slapped over a few now and then."

"Ever kill a man with a punch to the jaw?"

"No, suh! Ah never killed a man nohow."

"Ever see a man killed with a punch to the jaw before?"

"No, suh; never seed it happen befo'."

"It must have been quite a punch."

"Ah'll say it was, boss man!"

"Did you ever, in all your ring experience, see a man hit as hard as that in the jaw?"

"No, suh. In all the fights Ah've seen everywhere, Ah never seed a punch lak that one befo'. Dat was de punch of punches."

"Did you see Dempsey knock out Willard in Toledo?"

Yas, suh; Ah sho' did."

"Was the punch with which the defendant killed Jake Mullin, in your opinion, as hard or harder than the punches with which Dempsey—"

"Your honor," Mr. Yistle irritably interrupted, "may I be enlightened on a point? Is this a murder trial or a debate on the relative merits of the world's greatest punchers?"

JUDGE BARLOW LOOKED at Gillian with twinkling eyes. The judge had one time remarked at a luncheon at the Lawyer's Club that he would rather see a good fight than eat.

"Perhaps," he gravely suggested, "Mr. Hazeltine has some intention of establishing a hypothetical point in connection with his defence."

"Your honor," Gillian returned, "I am tremendously curious. My questions are, I will admit, somewhat irrelevant to the issue. It has seemed to me that a scientific issue is involved. For my personal edification—and in the larger interests of science—I am anxious to ascertain whether or not the punch delivered by the defendant was or was not the most tremendous punch ever delivered by a prize fighter."

"I object strenuously," Mr. Yistle snapped, "to the pursuance of such an inquiry in this court room. The power of that punch was sufficient to kill a man. That has been proved. Legally, the issue is closed. I am certain that your honor and the gentlemen of the jury are not interested in the relative power of historic punches."

The expression on the face of Judge Barlow and on the faces of the twelve jurymen did not indicate that they agreed with Mr. Yistle.

Judge Barlow bent forward and said with an air of reluctance:

"Mr. Hazeltine, perhaps you would better confine your cross-examination to the issue at stake."

"Very well, your honor," said Gillian briskly. He faced the grinning witness. "Tiger, how many drinks had you had that evening before you went to the Black Cat with Mullin and Micky Welsh?"

"Objection!" roared Mr. Yistle.

"Overruled."

Gillian walked closer to the witness. "Isn't it true that you and Micky Welsh polished off a bottle of gin between you in Kid Murphy's dressing room? Don't lie, Tiger!"

"No, suh—yas, suh," the witness stuttered. "Mebbe Ah had—well, jes' a *drop*."

"A great big drop—about the size of your, fist?"

"Ah reckon so, boss man."

Mr. Yistle's face was crimson. He said furiously to Mr. Bullock: "Why in the devil didn't you find that out? It kills him as a witness!"

Mr. Bullock's Adam's apple bobbed up and down.

"Tiger," Gillian said fiercely, "you told me you had never killed a man, with your fist 'or nohow.' Wasn't that a lie? Didn't you once serve four years in Georgia for cutting a man's throat with a razor—"

"Lissen, lissen, boss man," the witness wailed, "Ah killed dat man. Sho' I did. But Ah—Ah was provoked. Dat man wuz fussin' around wid my woman. Ah wuz let off—"

"That's enough," Gillian stopped him. "Your honor, I respectfully request that the evidence of this witness be stricken from the record. His credibility is certainly impeachable."

Mr. Yistle did not even enter an objection. Judge Barlow turned to the stenographer and said:

"You will strike out the entire examination and cross-examination of this witness. Next witness!"

8

"THE PUNCH MURDER"

THE STATE'S NEXT witness was John Grant, the head waiter at the Black Cat. He was a furtive-eyed individual and he had a guilty look. In response to Mr. Yistle's questions, he stated that he had just conducted the party containing Jake Mullin, Tiger and Mickey Welsh to the table when Bunce came running over and struck Mullin a terrific blow in the jaw.

"We won't go into the terrific nature of that blow," said the district attorney dryly. "We are merely interested in whether or not you saw or heard any provocation on the part of the deceased which would have justified the defendant in striking that blow. Did you or did you not?"

"I did not," stated Mr. Grant, with his eyes shifting about the ceiling.

"That will be all. Does the defence wish to ascertain just how powerful that blow was?"

The jury smiled. There was a ripple of amusement about the court room when Gillian asked:

"Mr. Grant, are you a fight fan?"

"I am. I go to all the big fights."

"Now, Mr. Grant, will you be so good as to indicate just where you were standing when the blow that killed Jake

Mullin was struck?" Gillian indicated the diagram of the Black Cat which had been admitted as Material Exhibit A for the State.

"I was standing there." The witness pointed.

"How far were you from the table at which Mullin was standing?"

"About twelve feet."

"You had shown Mullin and his guests to the table and were on your way away?"

"Yes, sir."

"So that when the blow was struck your back was toward Mullin?"

The witness suddenly lifted his eyes to the ceiling, again. "No, sir; I was backing away."

"As a servant backs out of the presence of royalty, for example?"

Mr. Yistle snapped; "Objection!"

The witness: "I was backing away!"

Mr. Hazeltine: "I wish the gentlemen of the jury to observe the little circles of white on this diagram. They indicate tables. These tables are, I believe, so close together that a man must squeeze sideways to pass between them. I want the witness to explain how he could have navigated—"

The witness: "I could do it in my sleep!"

Mr. Hazeltine: "Have you ever done it in your sleep?"

His honor: "Gentlemen! Mr. Hazeltine, what are you trying to prove?"

Mr. Hazeltine: "Merely, your honor, that the witness is a liar!"

Mr. Yistle: "Prove it!"

Mr. Hazeltine: "I think I have proved it."

THE WITNESS'S EYES were darting all about the room. He burst out now, in a whining voice; "I tell you, I saw Bunce punch Mullin in the jaw."

"He saw him!" Mr. Yistle exclaimed. "Your honor, I object to this pettifogging! If the defence has finished with this witness—"

"Not yet," said Gillian. "Mr. Grant, let us return to this punch. Whether you saw it out of the back of your head or not, is not the question. I want to know if that punch was, in your opinion, of sufficient force to kill a man."

"Yes, it was!"

Did you, in all the years of your attendance of prize fights, ever see a punch to equal it?"

"No, sir!"

"Would you compare it in violence to the kick of a vicious horse?"

The witness: "All I know, it was a terrible punch, I never saw a horse kick a man in the jaw."

"But it was the most terrific punch you ever saw?"

"That's what I said."

"There was nothing accidental about it, was there, Mr. Grant? I mean, it didn't strike you that the punch was a trick punch?"

"No—it was a straight uppercut, or a plain uppercut, nothing else."

Very patiently but wearily Mr. Yistle broke in: "Your honor, I submit that every word of this cross-examination is immaterial and therefore inadmissible as evidence."

"So do I, your honor," Gillian cheerfully agreed. "Also, every word of the direct examination. I insist that this witness is a liar. I insist that he was walking away, not backing away, and that he could not have seen that punch."

The witness said angrily: "Well, I heard it, didn't I?"

Gillian pounced on that. "Did you?"

"I did!"

"What did it sound like?"

"It sounded like somebody breaking a plank across his knee."

"I submit, your honor," said Gillian, "that the entire testimony of this witness be held inadmissible to the record."

Judge Barlow said promptly: "It is so ordered. In my mind there is a grave question that this witness actually saw that punch delivered."

Gillian grinned at Mr. Yistle, and the district attorney glared. Judge Barlow adjourned the court for luncheon. In the babble that followed this order, Mr. Yistle strode over to Gillian.

"Don't think for a minute," he snarled, "that you've got my goat. I've got this case sewed up tight. As usual, you are making a travesty of the defence. Just as I said, you are trying to turn this court room into a three-ring circus. If necessary, I can produce six dozen witnesses who saw Bunce strike that blow. And if you goad me into it, I'll do it."

"I wonder," said Gillian dreamily, "if any of them are reputable. Tell me, Bert, have you honestly one reputable witness?"

"I'll show you," sputtered the district attorney.

Gillian, grinned and walked away. He sought an obscure restaurant where six per cent draft beer was served; and proceeded to entertain eight reporters while he ate. Why, they unanimously wanted to know, was he hammering away on the murderous quality of the punch that had killed Jake Mullin?

"I will come clean with you," said Gillian. "I am out to prove that that was a superhuman punch—so powerful that no living man could have struck it!"

The eight reporters made sarcastic remarks. It was hinted that Mr. Hazeltine had an ax concealed in his sleeve.

"Hasn't he always?" cried Green, of the *Mirror*.

"Why bother about my motive?" Gillian jovially asked. "Isn't that punch giving you boys a story? Can't you illustrate it with drawings of other famous punches of history?"

"Is Kitty Kelly going to take the stand?" asked Burke of the *News*.

"Yes."

"Who are the other defence witnesses?"

"I can't answer that."

A very youthful and inexperienced reporter asked: "Mr. Hazeltine, do you think you have a chance of getting Bunce off?"

His seven contemporaries burst into laughter.

THE EARLY AFTERNOON editions of the tabloids contained the statement, over her photograph, that Kitty Kelly would take the stand for the defence. The widow of Jake Mullin had been in seclusion since the murder. She had, the tabloids truthfully said, been accessible to no one but Gillian.

The afternoon session was devoted to six more eye-witnesses to the blow that had felled and killed Jake Mullin. Each testified emphatically that Jake Mullin had said nothing, done nothing, to provoke the blow that had ended his life. Mr. Yistle was piling up evidence to establish beyond all doubt that the blow had not been struck in self-defence. Gillian devoted himself to heckling the witnesses, or, as Mr. Yistle described it so bitterly, pettifogging. He also questioned each witness as to the power of that blow. Was it as powerful as the kick of a vicious horse?

One enterprising tabloid published a "composite photograph," showing an agonized Jake Mullin being simultaneously struck by the fist of a ferocious Battling Bunce and by the hoof of a horse, with the caption, "Which Delivers the Greater Blow?"

The punch that killed Mullin was being referred to by the press more and more as "the greatest punch in history," "the most terrific punch ever delivered by a human." The tabloids began to refer to the case as the "Punch Murder."

Gillian instructed his secretary to start a scrap book of such clippings.

On the morning of the second day of the trial, the State produced six more eye-witnesses, each of whom, in turn, Gillian heckled until the court room was in an uproar. Mr. Yistle referred bitterly to his clowning. He resented the fact that the Punch Murder case was resolving itself into almost uncontrollable laughter.

When Gillian put the question to any witness, "Would you say that that punch was as powerful as the kick of a horse?" it was impossible for the bailiffs to restore order for sometimes as long as ten minutes. Only when Judge Barlow reluctantly threatened to have the court room cleared did Gillian desist. But the humor of the situation had escaped bounds.

Once Mr. Yistle roared at Gillian: "Are you attempting to have this case laughed out of court?"

Gillian solemnly answered; "It is my serious opinion that it deserves to be laughed out of court."

No one seemed to mind Gillian's tactics except Mr. Yistle, Mr. Bullock and the accused. Battling Bunce was worried. Why, he wanted to know, wouldn't the jury laughingly return a verdict of guilty? It didn't strike *him* as funny. Not much.

"I thought you didn't care whether you were electrocuted or not," Gillian once flashed at him. "Have you changed your mind?"

"I don't want to die," stated Battling Bunce.

On the afternoon of the second day of the trial the State rested. Twenty witnesses to that now nationally famous punch had taken the stand. And it was the opinion of the press that Gillian Hazeltine did not have a case; that he was making merry at the expense of a doomed man.

9

THE CASE FOR THE DEFENCE

"IS THE DEFENCE ready?"

"The defence is ready, your honor."

Gillian arose from the counsel table and walked toward the jury. Perhaps ten feet from the box he stopped, folded his arms, and looked along the two lines of expectant faces. The entire court room seemed to hold its breath as he began.

"Gentlemen of the jury, you have heard the testimony given by a formidable array of witnesses, proving beyond the slightest doubt that Jake Mullin was struck in the jaw by the defendant with such force that, time after time, that blow has been compared to the kick of a killer horse.

"You heard one witness solemnly declare that the sound of the blow was comparable to that made when a plank is broken. Another, perhaps humorously, compared the sound to that of a safe falling from the top of a ten-story building upon a concrete sidewalk. What we have learned from this testimony is that the defendant, with the most terrific punch probably ever delivered in the history of scientific punching, killed the light heavyweight champion of the world—Jake Mullin.

"All of that, we know, has been proved. It now devolves

upon me to prove to you that the human faculties in moments of great stress and excitement are prone to err. You have, gentlemen of the jury, doubtless heard accounts of conflicting testimony in so-called eye-witness reports to shootings. Of a given number of witnesses, no two will have heard the same number of shots fired; no two will agree upon the precise action which took place."

Gillian took a step nearer the jury box. His steel-blue eyes seemed to bore into the souls of the twelve jurymen. There was no humor about the famous criminal lawyer now. He was deadly in earnest.

"Gentlemen of the jury," he went on in hushed tones, "has it ever occurred to you to ask why, among such witnesses, not one of them saw the event precisely as it happened? Why?" Gillian repeated. "Let me tell you why! Because, but of a dozen witnesses, out of a dozen dozen such witnesses, not one of them saw it clearly! Why did not one of them see it clearly? Because not one of them was a *trained observer!*"

Again Gillian paused. Again the quiet was so profound that a fly could be heard buzzing against a windowpane.

"Why was it," Gillian demanded in a sharper voice, "that of the twenty witnesses whose testimony you heard, each and every one of them overlooked the trifle that most counted—a tremendous trifle? Why? Because these witnesses were scared, excited, rattled; because not one of them is a trained observer."

Gillian again hesitated. Mr. Yistle looked at his yes-man and whispered: "I knew it! I knew he would spring something like this! But he can't get away with it!"

"No, sir!" breathed Mr. Bullock.

"My first witness," said Gillian, "will be Finister Chardon."

Mr. Yistle's eyes became round and slightly bulging. So did Mr. Bullock's. There was an audible stir at the press table.

FINISTER CHARDON, BLAND and imperturbable, walked up to the witness chair and sat down. Duly sworn, Mr. Chardon stated in answer to Gillian's rapid questions that he was the vice president of the Greenfield First National.

"In the past few years," Gillian said, "is it not true that you have become tremendously interested in rooting out the social and civic evils which exist in our city?"

Mr. Chardon admitted, with a smile, that this was indeed true.

"Is it not true, Mr. Chardon, that you took active steps which resulted in the suppression of cheap dance halls where the morals of the voting women of Greenfield's working class were exposed to the most insidious temptations?"

"That is true, Mr. Hazeltine."

"Is it not true, Mr. Chardon, that you were personally responsible for stamping out of existence seven or eight bootleg dives where liquor, proved to contain wood alcohol, was being sold?"

"Yes, that is true, Mr. Hazeltine."

Gillian picked up a sheet of paper from his table, glanced at it, and put it down again.

"Mr. Chardon, on the night of June twentieth last, did you visit the Greenfield auditorium with the view of seeing for yourself whether or not prize fighting would demoralize the youth of this community?"

"I did, Mr. Hazeltine."

"After the fights, did you not go to the Black Cat Club with a view to seeing for yourself how wicked this night club was?"

"I did exactly that, Mr. Hazeltine."

"Before you tell us what you saw there that night, I wish you would tell the jury whether or not you consider yourself a trained observer, an expert observer."

"That is a question," answered the reformer, "which puts a severe strain on my modesty. I will answer it in this way: My research work has made it absolutely necessary for me to develop the highest powers of observation. I must overlook no detail. I must see not only the whole picture, but the most trivial items which go to make the picture."

Gillian saw Mr. Yistle suddenly smile and lean over to whisper to his yes-man.

He saw Mr. Bullock smile delightedly and nod his head.

"Now, Mr. Chardon," said Gillian, "will you describe what you saw in the Black Cat Club on the night of June 20 in connection with the murder of Jake Mullin?"

"I saw it all clearly," said the reformer. "I was sitting within five feet of Jake Mullin when the blow was struck which killed him."

Several of the jurymen leaned forward. Mr. Yistle nervously stood up. He began fiddling with his gold watch fob as he always did when he was nervous.

"I had just been seated at my table—" Mr. Chardon continued.

"Kindly indicate on this diagram which table it was. The red circle indicates the table to which Mullin's party had been conducted by the head waiter."

Mr. Chardon leaned forward and indicated with his long forefinger one of the adjoining black circles. "That was the table."

"Proceed, Mr. Chardon," said Gillian.

"I was seated at this table I have indicated when Mr. Mullin, a colored man and a red-haired man, who I later learned were Tiger Wales and Micky Welsh, prize fighters, were ushered up by the head waiter."

THE REFORMER PAUSED and cleared his throat. His bright little eyes traveled along the jury's faces.

"I was keenly interested in fighters, and I was taking particular note of every detail of Jake Mullins costume, which consisted of a tan suit, a maroon vest and a grass-green necktie, when I saw him turn and glance sharply across the room, then beckon. A moment later, this young man who is sitting at the table there—" he indicated Battling Bunce. "That young man came hastening over in answer to Mullin's beckoning finger. He beckoned like this."

The witness held out his hand, palm up. He doubled up all of the fingers of the hand, but the forefinger. This he then rapidly crooked several times.

"There was a great deal of confusion," stated the reformer. "People who had recognized the light heavyweight champion and his two friends were shouting at them, but I was so close that I overheard every word that Mullin and Bunce said."

Mr. Chardon paused again. Gillian said gravely:

"Tell the jury just what was said, Mr. Chardon."

"When Bunce came up," the reformer obliged, "Mullin said to him, 'So this is where you are, you dirty little crook!

I'll teach you to horn in where I am. I am going to knock you for a row of ashcans.' With that, he doubled up his right fist and drew it back to strike. But quicker than anything I have ever seen in my life, Bunce struck him!"

"Did Bunce say anything to him, Mr. Chardon?"

"Yes, Mr. Hazeltine. As he struck the blow, he exclaimed: 'Call me a crook to my face, will you?'"

"Thank you, Mr. Chardon. Does the State wish to cross-examine this witness?"

MR. YISTLE FAIRLY sprang at Finister Chardon. He began firing questions at him. He demanded that Mr. Chardon prove his contention that he possessed exceptional powers of observation by describing in detail the decorations in the Black Cat Club. He attacked his description of the scene between Mullin and Tim.

"You might have memorized all this!" he shouted. Mr. Yistle was perspiring freely. He knew that this one witness, because of his unquestioned standing in the community, was more credible than his twenty witnesses. He knew that Finister Chardon was lying. But how could he prove it?

Gillian was fully aware of what was going on in Mr. Yistle's mind.

"Your honor," said Gillian sharply, "I object to the bull-dozing tactics being employed by the district attorney. The witness has amply proved that he is an expert observer."

"He has not proved it to *my* satisfaction!" declared Yistle.

"Then," said Gillian quickly, "let's give him a test. Mr. Chardon," he said before Mr. Yistle could cut in, "we want to give your powers of observation an impromptu test. You claim, do you, that you never miss a detail of any scene?"

The witness smiled deploringly. "I would not go so far as that, Mr. Hazeltine. I am not infallible."

"Tell us," snapped Gillian, "everything you saw when you walked into the courthouse this morning. But first—are you a frequent visitor of the courthouse?"

"No, Mr. Hazeltine; this is my first visit here in three or four years. Let me think. I will begin with the courthouse doors." Mr, Chardon began with the courthouse doors. He described them in infinite detail, their ornate bronze handles, their protruding bronze hinges, their bronze filigree panels. He described the entrance hall, the doors leading from it, the legends painted on these doors, the bulletin board, and the announcements on the bulletin board. Step by step, detail by detail, he described his progress into the courthouse.

It took him a full half hour. Long before he had finished, the eyes of the jurymen were full of wonderment. It was an amazing demonstration of the powers of observation. And it had taken Finister Chardon an entire week of evenings to memorize this list of details which Gillian had supplied him!

When he had finished, Mr. Yistle said in a venomous low voice to Gillian: "That was a clever trick, but it was a circus trick." And to Judge Barlow: "Your honor, may I recall some witnesses? I wish to reopen their testimony on certain points this witness has raised."

"Is this witness excused?"

"Yes, your honor."

"He may wait," said Gillian, "for further examination."

Mr. Yistle recalled Mike Flaherty, the policeman who had made the arrest. He recalled other witnesses. They stuck to their stories. Gillian then recalled Finister Chardon. He stuck to his story. It seemed that a deadlock had been reached. Then Gillian put Kitty Kelly on the stand.

THE WIDOW OF Jake Mullin, dressed in black, went slowly to the stand. Her face was covered by a heavy black veil which she did not raise until she was seated. And when she raised it, the court room gasped.

Kitty Kelly was beautiful, and this was the beauty of infinite sadness. She was a Madonna. Her large lovely blue eyes gazed sadly, almost reproachfully, at the jury.

Her voice was sad, but it was sweet and clear. She spoke slowly but without hesitation.

"I want you to tell me," said Gillian gently, "the story of Timothy Bunce. I want you to spare no details, Kitty."

The girl told the story. She told it simply; of Tim's courtship, of her discovery that he had in him the makings of a great fighter. She told of her meeting Jake Mullin, and of the bullying tactics her father and brothers had employed to force her to marry him. She described Mullin's meanness and his brutality.

When Mr. Yistle tried to interrupt, the jury glared at him. Even the judge glared at him. Gillian plied his questions skillfully. He presently set an example and pulled out a large white linen handkerchief with which he dabbed at his eyes. Three men on the jury presently produced handkerchiefs. And the tragic story went on. All through the court room could be heard the nervous clearing of throats. The sad voice said in conclusion:

"I am not sorry that Jake Mullin is dead. He met his death justly." She stopped.

Gillian said huskily: "That will be all. Thank you, Kitty."

Mr. Yistle, who had seen, in this girl's appealing sadness, his efforts wiped away, leaped to his feet and cried:

"It's true, isn't it, that you are still in love with this—this red-handed murderer?"

And the blue-eyed girl said simply: "Of course it's true. I love Tim. I will always love him. He is the only man I could ever love."

"Yes, yes, yes!" snarled the district attorney. "And it's true, isn't it, that you would lie yourself black in the face to save him from the electric chair?"

"Of course I would lie, if it would save him," Kitty Kelly answered in that sweet, sad voice that Gillian had worked so hard with her to perfect. "But I haven't had to lie." She stretched out her hands in a quick little appealing gesture. "Who wants poor Tim to die—do you?"

The court room broke into an uproar. That faltering little question was Gillian's master stroke. How many times had he rehearsed Kitty in delivering that faltering little question, with just the proper accent, with that pathetic lowering of the eyes when it had been said? Kitty had been a difficult subject. She had wanted to go on the witness stand and fight for Tim.

Mr. Yistle sat down. He was trying to discuss the crumbling of their case with Mr. Bullock. Mr. Bullock was evidently devoid of ideas.

"The defence rests!"

Mr. Yistle was too angry to talk coherently to the jury. He tried. He could only sputter. Gillian, in his address, spoke feelingly of the great love that existed between these two splendid young people: "A love that would last beyond the electric chair, if you could find it in your hearts to send this splendid young man to such a doom—a love that would last beyond the grave."

It was once said of Gillian that he could play upon the emotions of a jury just as Kreisler plays upon the violin. That afternoon, certainly, he demonstrated his greatness as a jury lawyer.

Mr. Yistle, in his closing argument, begged, entreated, implored, commanded the jury to keep their heads; to apply logic to this situation, not mawkish sentimentality. But their minds seemed to wander.

The jury was out ten minutes. When they returned with a verdict, the foreman announced it in a voice that rang with triumph.

"How say you?"

"Not guilty!"

MR. YISTLE—A PALE, thoroughly infuriated Mr. Yistle— came striding over to Gillian.

"You are," he snapped, "a disgrace to your profession!"

"Who won this case?" Gillian calmly returned.

"That is not the point! You got this man, this red-handed murderer off, with lying and pettifoggery and chicanery. Chardon was lying. Tell me he wasn't lying, damn you! You had something on him! You forced him to take the stand and lie. Tell me you aren't a blackmailer!"

"I wouldn't dream of it," said Gillian.

"And that girl," Mr. Yistle panted, "now that you've taught her how to act, why don't you put her on the stage?"

"Her husband might object," said Gillian. And in answer to Mr, Yistle's expression of pained bewilderment which had joined his expression of baffled fury, Gillian said: "You see, Bert, the newspaper boys have been mighty generous to me. I wanted them to have a nice meaty piece of news for their afternoon editions—to sweeten up the news of the verdict. So I staged a marriage back in the jail during the noon recess."

Gillian turned his muscular back on the district attorney. Battling Bunce was busily shaking hands. Under his left arm was clamped the book of press clippings which Gillian's secretary had carefully compiled and which Gillian had given the young man early this morning. On the cover of the book was neatly stamped, in gold, the title:

A Punch Like the Kick of a Horse!

"Come with me," said Gillian. "We have an important engagement. Kitty is waiting in my car. Let's get out of here."

During the ride to Gillian's office, Battling Bunce said not a word. He held his wife's hand tightly and gazed raptly at the back of the chauffeur's neck. That amazing volume entitled "A Punch Like the Kick of a Horse!" he held tightly in his other hand.

In Gillian's private office, Paddy Tobin and another man were waiting. The other man was Frankie Walsh, heir presumptive to the light heavyweight throne; a superior young man with large white teeth, a hard grin, and the shoulders of a bull. He was sprawled in a chair and he did not arise.

Gillian closed the door and said: "Well, Paddy?"

Frankie Walsh spoke before Paddy could part his lips.

"It's a lot of hooey," he stated "I'll fight Tim, because the sport writers all over the country have gone cuckoo over this 'punch like the kick of a horse.' It'll draw a big gate, but there won't be no fight."

"No?" said Battling Bunce. "How do you figure that out, Frankie?"

"How? Because you ain't got a punch. I saw you with Kid Murphy. I don't know how you killed Jake Mullin, but it wasn't with any punch—unless you had a horseshoe in that hand."

"Do you hear him, Paddy?" demanded Battling Bunce.

"Sure, Tim. You go right on talking to him."

"I'll talk to him!" snapped the Battler. "So you think I haven't got a punch, do you? Well, lemme tell you something, Big Boy. I have a punch like the kick of a horse—and I don't need any horseshoe. I have got the greatest punch that ever went into any ring."

"Is that so?" said Gillian mildly.

"You bet it's so! I've got a greater punch than Jack Dempsey ever had! I'll take you, Walsh, in just one round, I used to think all my knock-outs were accidents. I even thought that that punch that killed Mullin was an accident. I know better now. I have probably the greatest punch in history. And when I meet you, Walsh, I'll prove it. Will I, Paddy?"

"You sure will, kid."

THE BACKING UP of that promise is, of course, history. Gillian and Vee Hazeltine journeyed to New York to occupy first row ringside seats at the brief but exciting encounter which placed the light heavyweight crown upon the very immodest head of Battling Bunce. They saw Battling Bunce, a human tiger, leap from his corner when the bell rang for that historic first round. They saw him batter Frankie Walsh about the ring with terrific punches until Frankie Walsh collapsed, unconscious—with half of the round still to go!

And in his dressing room later, Gillian experienced sensations not unlike those which Frankenstein suffered when the monster he had created became uncontrollable.

"Well, Mr. Hazeltine, did I show that palooka whether I have a punch or not? Did I show that crowd that I have a punch like the kick of a horse?"

"You did," Gillian agreed.

"Did I show the world that I have the greatest punch that ever went into the ring?"

"I guess you did, Tim,"

"I'll take 'em all," stated the Battler. "I only wish Dempsey was in his prime. I only wish Tunney would come back. In another year or so, I will be in the heavyweight division. Watch my dust!"

Later that evening, Gillian had a word with Kitty Kelly Bunce alone. The change in her was startling. The Madonna of the witness stand had become a bright-cheeked, merry-eyed girl. She was happy, but she was troubled.

"I don't mind it, Mr. Hazeltine," she said. "Tim is good, and I'm glad he's cured of his modesty, and knows he's good. But sometimes I get a little tired hearing about it. Have you—have you a cure for boastfulness?"

www.ingramcontent.com/pod-product-compliance
Lightning Source LLC
Chambersburg PA
CBHW072356030726
47505CB00014B/1849